MW00935272

Praise for
The Mystery of the Golden Ball

"Readers will devour this adventure with Pen and Quin as they solve a mystery and share their love of soccer." ~ Donna Feyen, Founder of www.MoreThanAReview.com

"Move over Encyclopedia Brown, new detectives are in town. Twins Penelope and Quintus are back, cracking their second case. Brisk pacing, likable characters, and a compelling plot make for a winning sequel that's sure to leave mystery and sports fans cheering for more." ~ Kristin L. Gray, author of Vilonia Beebe Takes Charge and Koala Is Not A Bear

OTHER TITLES BY KS MITCHELL

Pen & Quin: International Agents of Intrigue

The Mystery of the Golden Ball

KS Mitchell

Copyright ©2020 Kimberly Mitchell
Cover copyright © 2020 Elaina Lee/For the Muse Designns
Interior Design and Formatting by Woven Red Author Services,
www.WovenRed.ca

First Edition

Printed and bound in the United States of America. All rights reserved. No part
of this book may be reproduced or transmitted in any form or by any means,
electronic or mechanical, including photocopying, recording, or by an
information storage and retrieval system-except by a reviewer who may quote
brief passages in a review to be printed in a magazine, newspaper, or on the
Web-without permission in writing from the publisher. For information,
please contact Vinspire Publishing, LLC, P.O. Box 1165, Ladson, SC 29456-
1165.

All characters in this work are purely fictional and have no existence outside
the imagination of the author and have no relation whatsoever to anyone
bearing the same name or names. They are not even distantly inspired by any
individual known or unknown to the author, and all incidents are pure
invention.

ISBN: 978-1-7341507-5-9

For Mom and Dad. Thank you for everything,
including all the soccer practices and games.

1

Thwack! The soccer ball flew past Quin's diving body and hit the back of the net with a satisfying smack. He pushed himself up from the ground and glared at his sister.

"Nice shot, Pen," Coach Sikes called. "Keep it up and we'll win the league again."

Pen shot a devilish smile at Quin. "Thanks, Coach." She walked up to her twin brother. "Too bad we'll have to look for a new keeper."

Quin pulled the ball out of the goal and glared at her. "It's the first practice, and I haven't played all summer. Broken arm. Remember?" He held up one gloved hand and pointed to his right arm. He'd broken it at the beginning of the summer, falling out of a tree to save his sister's life.

Pen shook her head, whipping her long, dark ponytail back and forth. "Excuses won't make a difference when we play in the Friendship Cup. I thought you said your arm felt better."

Quin scowled and shoved the ball into his twin's hands. "It does. Bet you can't do that again."

She grinned. "You're on, *hermano*, if you think you can stop me."

Coach Sikes blew the whistle and motioned them in. The twins sprinted from the goal to the sideline. St. Mary's sat on a small hill above the field. Tomorrow it would be full of students for the first day of school, but today only the teachers walked its halls, and Sister Doris, who watched the soccer practice from the cement steps leading down to the field. The team had soccer practice before classes began so the St. Mary Saints could get ready for the Friendship Cup, an international tournament being held in their hometown of Boston.

A tall girl carefully picked her way down the crumbling concrete steps and joined the team at midfield. The sun shone off a few highlights in her dark blond hair. She wore short green soccer shorts with a bright yellow shirt. Even from here, Quin recognized the Brazilian team jersey. She looked like she could run up and down the field without getting one hair out of place. Large tortoiseshell sunglasses shielded her eyes from the team, like a superstar avoiding the paparazzi.

"Team, this is Mariana da Silva," Coach Sikes said. "She just enrolled at St. Mary's and is joining our team."

"We already held tryouts." Quin heard the edge in his sister's voice. Since St. Mary's didn't have a girl's soccer team, girls could try out alongside the boys for the boy's team. Pen and eighth-grader Lyla Thompson were the only girls to get a spot this year, spots they worked hard to keep. Lyla nodded in agreement.

"Mariana played striker for her old team, Club Santos, in Brazil. She led them to a championship as their leading scorer. She doesn't need to try out," Coach Sikes said.

Quin's jaw dropped. A Brazilian player who played the same position as Pen for one of the best clubs in Brazil? Not good news for his sister. Not at all.

"Club Santos," Michael Blalock said. "Are you as good as Pelé?" He laughed but crossed his arms and stared at the girl. Quin and Michael had been best friends since kindergarten and he could practically hear Michael's thoughts behind his blond curls and the perpetual smirk on his face. Could this pretty new girl actually play soccer?

The coach patted Mariana on the shoulder. "I know the whole team will make you feel welcome. She's working on her English skills, too. Maybe you should get to know Pen and Quin here." The coach gestured to the twins. "They speak Spanish."

"They don't speak Spanish in Brazil," Pen said stiffly.

Mariana cocked her head and spoke for the first time. "She is right," she said, her accent thick. "We speak *Português* in my country. It is like," she paused and licked her lips. "Like Spanish and French and Italian all together. The most beautiful language in the world." One side of her mouth turned up into a partial smile.

"And beautiful people," Michael said. "Ouch." He rubbed the back of his calf where Pen had kicked him.

Quin shook his head. His sister and his best friend had been at each other's throats as long as he could remember.

"Let's get back to work. The tournament is only a few weeks away." Coach Sikes clapped his hands and gestured for them to go back to their drills.

Quin trotted back to the goal, his mind on the tournament. Since he'd gotten the cast off his arm, he'd trained extra hard with Pen, Michael, and sometimes with his older brother, Archie, when he came home from college at MIT. Still, a dull ache came from deep within his arm.

He took his position in the goal and waved for the rest of the team to start the drill. He groaned when Pen, Michael, and Mariana stepped up. He'd hoped for an easier lineup. At least he'd see what kind of player the new girl was. The three forwards started to do a triangle weave, where each player passes the ball to one of the other two and then sprints after the ball to take up a new position.

Pen blasted a pass to Mariana, but the Brazilian girl reached it easily and sent it smoothly back to Michael. As they neared the goal, Quin held his hands out low and shifted into position, waiting for the shot. He hoped his twin wouldn't take it. She'd purposefully been aiming all her shots at his weak side.

Mariana took the last pass, tapped the ball in front of her once, then sent it spinning toward the goal. Quin knew even as he stretched out in a dive he couldn't reach this shot. As gravity pulled him back down to the ground, he saw the ball slot neatly into the upper right corner of the goal.

The rest of the team erupted in cheers. Quin sighed and sat up. The other Saints all sprinted to clap Mariana on the back. All except for Pen.

She walked into the goal and kicked the ball hard into the net. "Not even Salvatore Cienfuegos could've saved that one."

Quin's all-time favorite goalkeeper, Salvatore Cienfuegos, played for Valencia.

"Maybe not." He wasn't sure the redheaded goalkeeper wouldn't have saved it. Cienfuegos was a magician in the air. "At least she won't be shooting at me during a game." He rolled to his feet and stretched out his arm.

"No," Pen said, her face dark. "She may be playing my position."

Quin frowned and watched Mariana jog back to midfield. Beyond the end of the field, a man leaned against a tree, watching the team practice. The man's features were lost under the shade of the tree.

"Who's that?" Quin gestured toward the man.

"Hopefully not another Brazilian striker," Pen grumbled. She followed Quin's gesture and shrugged. "I don't know. A parent?"

"He could be the coach of another team spying on our practices for the tournament."

Pen shook her head. "I doubt other coaches are interested in us. I heard Coach Sikes tell Michael's mom we're only in the tournament because they wanted to invite a local team. But I like the way you're thinking."

Quin rolled his eyes. After breaking his arm solving the mystery of the Codex Cardona, a missing Aztec painted book, he'd shot down all of his sister's ideas on how to revive their investigations into international intrigue. As far as he was concerned, solving one mystery was enough. For the rest of his life. His twin had other ideas.

The man seemed to feel the twins' eyes on him. He turned toward them and held their gaze. A large black jacket couldn't quite cover his bulky form. Who needed a jacket on one of the last days of summer?

"Whoever he is, we should tell Coach." After spending the summer tracking down an ancient painted book for Abuelito, being chased by an art thief, and falling out of a tree, Quin suddenly took all those warnings about strangers more seriously. "He doesn't look like a soccer coach."

Thwack. Another ball hit the back of the net, catching both twins by surprise. Three more teammates cheered.

"Grey Reyes," Coach Sikes shouted. "If you're just going to stand there, switch with Leary." Quin sighed and let Dennis Leary, the scrawny fifth-grade backup keeper, take his position in goal.

"Nice job," he muttered to Pen. "Now I might not be playing, either."

A loud buzzing interrupted them. Quin's phone lay behind the goal next to his water bottle. Quin still hadn't adjusted to carrying it with him all the time, but he'd decided after their last mystery it was better to keep it close.

Quin relinquished the goal to Dennis and picked up the phone, squinting to see the screen in the sunlight.

"Even I don't check my phone during practice," his sister teased. "Who's texting you? Archie?"

"No." He held the phone up and squinted through his glasses. "It's that app I downloaded about the European soccer leagues. They send me news updates on all the players and teams."

"Oh." Pen didn't follow the professional teams as closely as Quin. "That man is gone. And what is Mariana doing?"

"Huh?" Quin looked up from the phone. The man in black had disappeared.

"What a show-off."

Quin thought he heard a hint of jealousy in his twin's voice. At center field, Mariana juggled a ball with her feet. The ball bounced from one foot to the other without touching the ground. Pen glowered at the new girl. Somehow, Quin doubted his sister would work hard to help Mariana feel welcome. He felt slightly sorry for her, but then again, Pen had spent all summer driving shots at him. He looked back at his phone as the soccer headlines updated.

"Look at this."

He held out his phone but his sister ignored it, her eyes downfield, where Michael and Mariana seemed to be having an in-depth conversation.

"Penelope." Using his twin's full name was the quickest way to get her attention and annoy her at the same time. He waved the phone at her.

"What?" Pen grabbed the phone and glanced at the screen. "What's so important you have to show me now? Did Luca break a scoring record?" Luca was the best soccer player in the world, and Quin's second favorite player behind Salvatore Cienfuegos.

"It's the Ballon d'Or."

Luca had won the golden ball, the trophy given to the best international soccer player of the year. He beat Salvatore Cienfuegos for the honor. Quin had gone back and forth for days feeling happy for Luca, who'd scored more goals than any other rookie in his first professional season, and annoyed no goalkeeper had ever won when Cienfuegos was an amazing player.

"The trophy? What about it?" Her eyes were on Michael and Mariana, not Quin. At midfield, Michael kicked a ball high into the air, then trapped it by sitting on it. Mariana tipped back her sun-streaked hair and laughed.

"If that girl thinks she's going to take my spot—" She didn't finish her threat.

Quin knew she and Michael had texted a lot over the summer, but he didn't know if they were interested in each other. He decided not to ask. He didn't need life to get more complicated between his twin and his best friend.

"Pen, could you listen for once?"

She sighed and faced Quin, arms across her chest. "What's so important we're missing practice for it?"

He stabbed a finger at his phone. "That's what I'm trying to tell you. It's the golden ball. The trophy's been stolen."

2

Pen didn't feel like talking after practice. Her mind replayed all seven goals Mariana had scored, every one of them like a highlight off the sports channel. Quin sat on the seat next to her, scrolling through his phone. She assumed he was searching for more information on the stolen golden ball.

The city bus began to climb the steep slopes from St. Mary's to their neighborhood. Pen checked her texts as the bus bumped along. One from Michael Blalock caught her eye.

Yo! Nice practice. Mariana's good!!

She frowned and decided not to reply. She had another text from Anna about the cute clothes she'd found shopping with her mom in New York and wishing she could wear them instead of St. Mary's standard blue polo and skirt tomorrow. Pen stopped reading halfway through. Best friend or not, she didn't care about Anna's new clothes.

She missed the intrigue from their summer in Mexico. Yes, she and Quin had gotten into a little danger, but everything had turned out okay in the end.

Her phone buzzed again. Another text from Michael.

I bet we win the tournament w/Mariana. Think any scouts will be there?

Pen shoved the phone deep into her soccer bag, fed up with both Michael and the new Brazilian girl. The bus rumbled up the hillside past old Victorian homes and remodeled apartment buildings that made up Mission Hill, their neighborhood. The twins exited at the stop closest to home and continued walking up the steep street. The twin spires of the Basilica of Our Lady of Perpetual Help, or the Mission Church as most people in the neighborhood called it, dominated the skyline. High-rise offices of the medical and technology centers added to the view, which Pen normally stopped to admire, but not today.

The Grey Reyes manor, as their father called it, was an architectural jumble of parapets, towers, second-story balconies, and overhanging eaves protecting triple-pane bay windows. Its peeling gray paint matched its name and the house sprawled across the lawn, surrounded by oaks and maples, and even an apple tree leftover from the days when Mission Hill was simply an apple orchard outside of Boston.

Pen pointed to the red car with chipped paint parked in front of the house. "Archie's home."

They hurried up the driveway, ignoring the sidewalk to the front porch for a worn pathway past huge blue hydrangeas and a climbing rosebush determined to conquer the entire side of the house. One of the thorns caught Pen's T-shirt and pricked her arm.

"Stupid roses." Mamá had asked her to trim the rosebushes this summer, but she hadn't gotten around to it. Pen wiped the pinprick of blood from her arm and licked her finger clean. The twins rounded the corner and pushed open the back door leading to the mudroom. They threw their soccer gear down in front of the washing machine, and hurried into the adjacent kitchen. Their older brother sat at the round kitchen table spooning peanut butter straight from the jar into his mouth.

"Mamá will kill you if she sees you doing that," Pen said.

"*Buenas tardes* to you, too." Archie's words came out

muted with his mouth full of peanut butter. He set the jar down and went to the drawer for another spoon. He grabbed the bread and they made peanut butter and honey sandwiches, drizzling the honey so it dripped from the bread to the table and they had to mop up the sticky drops with their fingers.

"Did you hear about the Ballon d'Or?" Quin smacked through the last of his sandwich and started making another.

Archie nodded and shoved the rest of his sandwich in his mouth. His hair had grown long over the summer. The black tips hung in his eyes and curled around his ears. He swept them away from his eyes.

"*Loco*. Did you hear what happened?"

The twins shook their heads. Archie grinned and took another bite, relishing the information he had.

"Tell us," Quin groaned.

"Luca was at a charity event in Madrid and someone broke into his apartment and stole the trophy."

"Who would steal the trophy?" Quin marveled.

"That trophy's worth millions," Archie said. It could have been anyone in the world."

Pen set her sandwich down. "Why do we have to keep talking about Brazilian soccer players? Who cares?"

Her big brother lifted one dark eyebrow in a way she often mimicked.

"*Qué pasó, hermanita*? Why do you suddenly hate the best foot-balling nation in the world?"

Pen glowered at her sandwich and shrugged. Her twin filled Archie in on soccer practice and Mariana's arrival. Archie leaned back in his wooden chair until it rocked on the back two legs.

"Mariana da Silva," he mused. "That name sounds familiar."

Quin shrugged. "It's the name of a half dozen footballers."

Archie nodded but pulled out his phone. Pen leaned

over and watched him type da Silva and Brazilian football into a search. An entire page of da Silvas popped up, but she zeroed in on the first entry.

"Luca!"

Quin leaned over the other two, peering over his glasses at the tiny text on the phone. "I didn't know Luca's last name is da Silva."

"I thought you knew everything about him," Archie teased.

"Those Brazilian players always use one name." Quin read the full name on the site. "Lucas Juan Carlos Andrade da Silva."

"No wonder he uses a nickname," Archie laughed. "Like us."

They all nodded, preferring their nicknames to Penelope, Quintus, and Archelaus. This is what happened when you had a world-renowned archaeologist for a mother.

"But Mariana can't be related to him," Quin said. "Luca's amazing. He scored fifty goals for Real Madrid last season. And six of those against Salvatore Cienfuegos."

Archie shook his head. "How do you remember those stats?"

Quin shrugged. He picked up Archie's phone and scrolled through the article.

"Hey, don't you have your own phone now?" Archie protested.

Quin ignored him. "It says da Silva is one of the most common names in Brazil. It's just a coincidence Mariana has the same last name as Luca."

"Sure, a coincidence." Pen dropped her forehead to the table and knocked it against the wood a few times. She didn't need a Brazilian soccer star stepping into her position, related to Luca or not. When she looked up, Archie gave her the crooked grin she loved.

"So what are you planning for the school year, Penhead? Some way to eavesdrop on Sister Doris or turn St. Mary's into an intelligence agency?"

"I do have an idea. Maybe you can help me get it ready after dinner."

"The family spy," Archie teased.

"Takes one to know one," Pen shot back.

"We don't have time for spying," Quin interrupted. "We're not supposed to be investigating anything."

Pen sighed. She'd had trouble getting Quin interested in anything but soccer after he'd broken his arm. But most good investigators worked in teams. She needed her partner back. Maybe this stolen trophy could bring their investigative skills back. Pen smiled as she pictured herself finding and returning the trophy to Luca.

"We have to practice for the tournament," her twin said. "Or did you forget about Mariana already?"

The smile dribbled like honey off Pen's face. *"Nunca,"* she said with the force of a shot on goal.

The backdoor opened and Maria Grey Reyes called out.

"Hola casa. Hello house." She walked into the kitchen with an armful of books and a bag of groceries. Her long black hair, the same hair Pen and Archie had inherited, clung in damp tendrils against her face and her magenta sundress showed off bronzed shoulders. She looked stunning, despite the August heat. Pen felt a tightness in her chest when she thought about her mother these days. She didn't believe she could ever be that beautiful or successful.

Mamá set the books on the table, the groceries on the counter and beamed at them. *"Todos mis hijos* together." She planted kisses on the tops of their heads. "Why are you eating sandwiches? You'll destroy your dinner."

"You mean we'll ruin it," Pen said. Occasionally, Mamá still used the wrong expressions in English, even though she'd lived in the U.S. a long time.

"No, I mean destroy, *hija.* Your father's bringing home Thai food. We're celebrating."

"Good, I'm starving." Quin stuffed the last of his second sandwich in his mouth. They all burst into laughter.

"What are we celebrating?" Pen asked.

"All the Grey Reyes family together before a new school year," Mamá said. "With no adventures or mysteries, just *futból* and school and computers and art."

The three Grey Reyes kids exchanged looks. "Right, sure, okay Mamá."

"Let's go take some shots against Quin before dinner," Archie suggested. "I hear his arm needs extra practice."

Pen thought about Mariana probably-not-related-to-Luca-the-world's-best-footballer da Silva and jumped up from the table.

"I'll go first."

3

St. Mary's held their welcome-back assembly in the gym the next morning. The students squirmed on hard bleacher seats and whispered to each other as Sister Doris droned on about school rules and expectations, dress code, and proper conduct. Even though school rules prohibited using cell phones, Quin glimpsed more than one phone out of a pocket or backpack. Two rows in front of him, two fifth graders whispered and pointed to the screen of one girl's phone. More than once Quin thought he heard someone whisper "spider."

He tugged on the collar of his blue polo, feeling his neck grow warm. His phone had buzzed that morning along with what looked like the entire school. The text came from an anonymous person named SPYder, and what it said sent whispers racing down the gym bleachers even as Sister Doris called the school to order. Quin didn't have to read the text again to know who sent it.

Do you have a problem that needs solving? Let SPYder help. Experts in art, language, science, math—we have your solution. SPYder will solve any case, big or small.

He flicked his eyes down the row to where Pen sat next to Anna Callahan, her dark hair loose around her shoulders, conveniently hiding her face. For once, his sister didn't have her phone in her lap. Guilty, Quin thought. Pen would have her phone out like every other student if she didn't already know what the text said. What had his twin started now?

"With a shortage of nuns as qualified teachers, we've hired new teachers this year," Sister Doris said. Quin's ears perked up. New teachers? The gym buzzed as two hundred and fifty students all whispered at once.

"Quiet, please." Sister Doris surveyed the gym with her infamous, I-know-what-you're-thinking look. Combined with the severity of her traditional black robes, kids usually confessed on the spot. "This year sixth, seventh, and eighth grades will be taught by our newest additions to St. Mary's. Teachers, please stand."

Pen shifted in her seat and raised her eyebrows at him. He read her thoughts immediately. The new teachers were definitely younger than St. Mary's usual staff. Maybe this school year wouldn't be so terrible after all. He frowned and pointed at his phone. "SPYder?" he mouthed, hoping his sister shrugged or looked as puzzled as the rest of the students. Instead, Pen smirked and looked away. Definitely guilty.

The students around him broke into applause. Quin looked around and started clapping. "What are we clapping for?" he whispered to Michael.

His best friend grinned. "We're welcoming our new teachers. I might think of a different way to welcome them." Quin shook his head. He couldn't worry about Pen's schemes and Michael's shenanigans at the same time.

One of the new teachers stepped up and held up his hand. "These are the names of my students," he called out cheerfully. He had wiry red hair and eyebrows so pale they were almost white. Quin had been so busy thinking about SPYder, he'd missed the new teacher's name. The man called out Michael's name and Anna Callahan. Quin tensed. He hated the roll call at the beginning of the year, when teachers read full names. Call me Quin, he tried to telegraph to the teacher.

"Quintus Grey Reyes," the teacher called out. "What a wonderful name," he added, loud enough for everyone to hear.

Quin's entire body felt hot. Why did his parents have to be so inventive with their children's names? He rose from the bleachers and walked down, feeling the seventh and eighth graders' eyes on him, since they were the only grades left in the gym now. "Quintus," one of the eighth graders hooted as he stepped onto the gym floor.

"Stuff it."

"What was that?" Quin's teacher asked, pausing in the roll.

"I-uh-nothing." Quin meekly joined the line and waved to Michael, who was near the front since his last name began with a B. Anna, standing behind Michael, waved back. Quin stopped waving, leaving his hand half up, half down. He hadn't meant to wave to Anna, but he didn't mind that she'd waved back. But did she think he was waving only to her and not to Michael?

"Who you waving to, Quintus?" another eighth grader called. "Sister Doris?" Laughter rippled through the group until Sister Doris hushed them. He stabbed the toe of his shoe into the gym floor and shook his head. Not the best start to seventh grade.

$$\rho$$

Pen sighed when Quin, Anna, and Michael were all assigned to Mr. Hardy's homeroom. She surveyed the students left in the seventh-grade class. Snooty Eileen Esposito sat a row ahead of her, whispering with two girls from her enclave. Mariana sat by herself on the end of the row. Her blonde hair glowed softly in the florescent lights of the gym and she seemed oblivious to a row of eighth grade boys who gaped at her and whispered to each other. Mariana looked up and gave Pen a tentative smile. Pen frowned. She couldn't be friends with the girl threatening to take her starting spot on the soccer team.

"Penelope Grey Reyes," Sister Doris called. She made her way down the bleachers to her new teacher. Ms. Morgan stood at the head of the line of seventh graders. She had short brown hair, a round face, and a turned up, mischievous-looking nose. She smiled as Pen joined the line.

Somebody bumped Pen from behind. She turned to find Eileen Esposito. It looked like the girl had spent the morning curling her hair. This year she'd opted for red and blonde highlights in her normally dull brown hair.

"Looks like we're in the same class this year. Sorry you'll have to be second-best in everything." Her cohorts twittered.

"Nice curls. Too bad you're not the prettiest girl in school anymore."

Eileen's mouth dropped open, but she recovered quickly. "If you're implying you are—"

"I'm not." Pen nodded behind them. Mariana da Silva had joined the line. She stood nearly a head taller than the rest of the class. She smirked, knowing Eileen would be thinking about Mariana all day.

In the classroom, Ms. Morgan assigned Pen a desk near the window in the back of the room. She felt relieved she could at least see the outside world while trapped inside all day. Mariana got the desk next to her. Eileen glared at them from two rows away. The new girl turned to Pen.

"What's her problem?"

Pen sighed. It looked like the Fates, as her Greek tutor, Kostas, would say, had decided to throw her and Mariana together.

"Don't worry about Eileen Esposito. She's jealous of you."

Mariana's eyes widened. They were a seafoam green, flecked with blue. Not fair, Pen thought.

"Jealous of what?"

Pen shook her head. Was this girl that clueless? "Everything." She remembered the goals Mariana had scored in their scrimmage yesterday.

"She doesn't know me." Mariana glanced away but not before Pen caught the brief sheen of wetness in her eyes. What did this girl have to be sad about?

"Class?" Ms. Morgan tapped a marker against the board. "Before we get started, I wanted to draw your attention to this." She uncapped the marker and wrote in neat letters.

Pen nearly gasped out loud. She bit her lip instead. Ms. Morgan had written the entire text she and Archie had sent to every student at St. Mary's on the board.

Do you have a problem that needs solving? Let SPYder help. Experts in art, language, science, math—we have your solution. SPYder will solve any case, big or small.

"Sister Doris alerted all the teachers about this text some of you might have received. In her words, St. Mary's is a place for serious study, not criminal capers. Furthermore, using the school's student contact list is a school violation, as students should only be contacted if there is an emergency."

Pen frowned and put her hand up. She couldn't help herself. Ms. Morgan looked at her new seating chart. "Yes, Penelope?"

"It's Pen, and what if a student has an emergency? Couldn't that be a reason to contact this…SPYder?"

Ms. Morgan half smiled. "While I admire your concern, Penelo—Pen, if a student truly has an emergency, she may contact our staff."

Eileen's hand shot into the air. "Ms. Morgan?" She waved her hand around. Ms. Morgan checked her chart again. "Yes, Eileen, and this is the last question."

"Isn't texting someone you don't know dangerous? SPYder could be a kidnapper."

Ms. Morgan nodded her head. "That's a concern. Recently the police informed Sister Doris that a few unseemly characters have been seen near the school. That's why we're trying to track down the person responsible for the text."

Pen hadn't thought about the strange man dressed in black they'd seen at the soccer field until now. Was he an unseemly character? She and Quin hadn't told anyone. She'd forgotten him after Mariana began scoring goals in practice.

"Now that's enough about our current intrigue, but what a great segue into our first assignment."

The entire class groaned and Ms. Morgan laughed. "You don't even know what it is yet. In seventh grade, we start off the year looking closely at the American Revolution. I bet most of you have already studied the britches off this subject, especially living right here in Boston, the heart of the Revolution."

Pen nodded along with her classmates. They'd all visited the most famous landmarks every year for field trips: the Old South Meeting Hall, where patriots debated the fairness of taxes imposed by the British and eventually launched the Tea Party; the Old North Church and its famous tower where lanterns were lit to send Paul Revere on his midnight ride; and of course, the Battle of Bunker Hill.

"Most of you know Benjamin Franklin was a statesman and an inventor, but how many of you know he was also a master of deception and one of our first spies?"

Pen sat up straight. She'd never heard a teacher talk like this before. Nobody else in the class made a noise. All eyes were on Ms. Morgan. She smiled slyly and turned to the board.

"All this talk about SPYder and secrets has gotten me thinking about our projects on the American Revolution. I know Mr. Hardy's class is doing group presentations."

Pen couldn't help it. She pulled a face expressing her disgust. She only liked group projects when it involved Quin or Archie. And sometimes not even then. Ms. Morgan happened to glance her direction. Pen froze and tried to assume her normal appearance, which was hard with a teacher watching. But Ms. Morgan only grinned.

"I've decided I'd like you all to express some of your own independence on this project." She chuckled at her joke. "I'd like each of you to investigate the American Revolution from a unique viewpoint, not the one we always hear. Maybe from the British point of view. Or the Native Americans who helped. Or the African Americans who fought in the war, free or slave. Or maybe someone here would like to look into the development of our intelligence network that helped us win the war. There are many viewpoints in history that are not always covered in the textbook."

Eileen's hand waved madly. Ms. Morgan sighed and nodded. "Yes?"

"But Sister Doris said spying is bad. And don't spies break laws? You don't want us to break laws, do you Ms. Morgan?"

Ms. Morgan gritted her teeth. Pen had the impression her teacher wanted to stick her tongue out at Eileen. She knew that feeling.

"Of course, I don't want you to break any laws. I'm encouraging you to look at the Revolution a little differently. If you like, you can imagine you're more of a reporter than a spy. Both uncover important information, only one is making information public and the other is keeping it private."

Pen leaned back in her seat. She'd always assumed she'd solve mysteries and crimes when she grew up. She hadn't considered ways to solve mysteries without being an investigator.

"So," Ms. Morgan continued brightly. "I'll give you a week to research what aspect of the Revolution you'd like to uncover," she flashed a brief smile at the wordplay, "and I'll expect your reports the week after that." The class groaned but Ms. Morgan waved them off.

"Oh, and I almost forgot, for those of you missing class for the soccer tournament, don't think that gets you out of the assignment." A second round of groans passed through the class.

"But think about what secrets you might uncover in our city, the heart of the Revolution. You could find more than a soccer trophy waiting for you."

Lunchtime couldn't come fast enough for Pen. It was hard to adjust to sitting in a classroom all day. Her mind wandered back to summer when she and Quin had tracked the missing painted book all the way to Spain. She'd been terrified at the time, but somehow the warm, late summer sunlight spilling through the window made the danger of capturing an international art thief fade away. Pen didn't realize the lunch bell had rung until Mariana tapped her on the shoulder.

"It must be good, your *sonho*."

Pen cocked her head. "My what?"

Mariana laughed, but she covered her mouth with her hand, as if afraid someone might see, even though the classroom quickly emptied of students. "*Sonho*. It means 'dream' in Portuguese."

"Oh. I don't speak any."

"I know, just Spanish. Like you said in practice yesterday."

"Well, not just Spanish." Pen was about to tell her she spoke Latin, Greek, and a few words from a hodgepodge of languages, but they'd reached the hallway.

"Hey," Michael Blalock called out as Mr. Hardy's class poured out of the room next door. "Race you to the cafeteria. But you both know I'm the fastest forward we've got."

"*Em seus sonhos*," Mariana called back. "In your dreams," she translated for Pen.

"I think I got it. Run." They sprinted down the hall, slowed to a walk to pass Sister Doris and her office, then rounded the corner and ran the rest of the way. When they arrived at the packed cafeteria, both girls were laughing and out of breath. They grabbed trays of food and Quin waved at them from a table in the corner.

"Come on." Pen motioned to Mariana with her hand. "You can sit with us."

At the table, Quin and Anna were talking excitedly about their new teacher.

"Mr. Hardy's great," Quin said. "He said he believes in an integrative approach, so when we study history, we're going to center everything around that period—reading, science, even art." His voice rose when he mentioned this point. "And we're starting with the American Revolution. He said I could replicate one of the famous paintings or even create my own."

"Great," Pen said. She caught Michael's eye and rolled hers. He snickered but spoke to Mariana when she sat down.

"How's your first day going?"

Mariana shrugged. "*Bom*, but I think this girl does not like me." She pointed to Eileen Esposito across the room. Michael didn't take his eyes off Mariana.

"*Bom*? That means 'good' in Portuguese, right?"

"*Sim*," Mariana answered, her carefully-shaped eyebrows rising slightly.

"And that's 'yes.'" Michael laughed. "I googled a few words last night."

Mariana gave Michael a small smile. Pen bit her lip and started to regret inviting Mariana to sit with them.

"Did your class talk about the text from SPYder?" Anna asked. "Mr. Hardy told us he thought the person who'd written it had a brilliant idea."

"Really?" Pen said. Quin shot her a dark look.

"He also said school was the wrong place for it," Quin added. "And if we get another text, we should let a teacher know immediately."

"Who do you think sent it?" Anna had her phone out. Pen leaned over and saw her own message glowing on the screen.

"Not me." Michael stuffed the rest of his sandwich into

his mouth so his words were mumbled. "I solve my own problems."

Pen decided it was time to change the subject. She didn't like the way her brother was looking at her. She didn't need him giving away their secret.

"Hey, did you hear anything else about the Ballon d'Or?"

"The balloon what?" Anna asked.

Quin launched into an extensive explanation of the world-famous trophy and its long list of winners. Pen tried to catch Anna's eye to poke fun at her brother's long-winded speech, but to her surprise, Anna leaned in, listening.

Pen switched her gaze to Mariana. The Brazilian girl picked at her spinach salad, lasagna, and hard slab of garlic bread. She tore the bread into tiny pieces and left them on the tray.

"And nobody knows what happened to the trophy," Quin concluded his speech. "Can you imagine how Luca feels? He planned on sending it to Brazil to make his fans happy and someone stole it instead."

"That's terrible," Anna agreed.

"Just a bunch of thieves," Michael said.

"Who?" Mariana's voice was tight and cold.

Quin, Anna, and Michael looked at her blankly. "Whoever stole the trophy," Michael said.

Mariana stood up. "I am not hungry." She left the table, her tray still next to Anna.

"What got into her?" Quin asked as they watched the Brazilian girl stalk out of the cafeteria.

"Girls." Michael shrugged off glares from Pen and Anna. He and Quin launched into an argument over the world's best players and their teams. Of course, Quin thought Salvatore Cienfuegos was the best, while Michael argued only a forward, a goal scorer, could be the best, so Luca had beaten out Salvatore Cienfuegos for the world's best player.

Pen slowly ate her own food and half listened to Anna

talk about her idea for the group project in Mr. Hardy's class. Around her, students sneaked looks at their cell phones and even dared a text or two until Sister Doris walked in for her usual hawk-eyed swoop of the cafeteria. Pen had left her phone in her locker, even though it felt strange not to have it with her. She thought she'd be too tempted to check for texts to SPYder during the day. Soon the bell rang, signaling the end of lunch. Pen grabbed Quin's arm as they headed back to class.

"Keep cool about SPYder."

"I am. You should have told me what you and Archie were up to."

Pen shrugged his suggestion off. Ahead of them, Mariana popped out of the girls' bathroom. Her eyes looked red and she held a tissue in her hand.

"Hey, what do you think is up with Mariana?" Quin asked. They watched the girl duck back into Ms. Morgan's classroom.

"I don't know." Pen pondered her quick exit from lunch.

"She's hiding something." Quin said this low enough only Pen could hear.

She stared at her twin and nodded. Sometimes he was more perceptive than anyone else she knew.

Quin seemed to realize what he'd said. "Forget about it. It's not our problem. See you later."

He caught up with Michael and entered Mr. Hardy's classroom. Pen let the rest of her classmates flow around her, then she stepped to the door and watched Mariana sit at her desk, her blond head down so her hair covered her red-rimmed eyes. Her hands gripped a tissue in a tight ball. Pen walked slowly to her seat and sat down, staring hard at the Brazilian girl. Mariana's eyes darted in her direction, then away, but not before a guilty look flashed through them.

Quin was right. Mariana da Silva was hiding something, and if there was a mystery to be solved, Pen wanted to be right in the middle of it.

4

After soccer practice, the twins huddled together in Pen's room, Pen in her swiveling chair, Quin perched on the end of her bed. Pen had the shades drawn, as usual, and the door shut, making him feel a little claustrophobic. He preferred the open windows of his art studio downstairs, or the large window overlooking the oak tree in his room. But Pen was wired for secrecy. She'd even told their parents they were working on their school projects. Pen had opened a couple of search windows on spies in the Revolution just in case Mamá or Dad walked in.

Pen showed Quin the new email address she'd set up to receive texts from SPYder so it couldn't be traced back to them.

"Archie helped you do this?" Quin said dubiously from the bed.

"No, I did it myself." He caught the hint of pride in her voice. "He just checked to make sure it would stay anonymous."

Quin leaned back on the bed. Something pressed into his back and he rooted around the unmade bed until he found one of her mystery books. He set the book on her nightstand. His sister was always looking for a mystery, whether in stories or real life.

"I thought you said the internet was never truly

anonymous."

Pen shrugged. "True, but you'd need someone like Archie to trace the account. Sister Doris won't have a clue how to do it." She tapped a key on her computer and then punched the air. "Alright! Three mysteries to solve already."

"What?" He hurried to her side. Three new messages sat in the inbox. He shook his head. "I can't believe this actually worked." Their adventure last summer led to a broken arm, but it could have easily been more. Quin shivered, remembering the cold voice of the art thief and the dark shadow of a gun in moonlight. Pen had asked him to keep SPYder secret. Why had he agreed?

"Of course it worked. Why wouldn't it?" Pen clicked on the first email and read it aloud.

> I forgot my locker combination and I'm too embarrassed to ask my teacher. How can I figure it out myself?

Quin burst out laughing, all thoughts of danger and darkness falling away. "Some international mystery that is."

His sister sighed. "This must be from a fourth grader." Only students in the upper grades were allowed to have lockers, starting with fourth grade.

"You did promise to answer all inquiries." He stifled a laugh at the perplexed look on her face. "So, how do you solve this problem?"

Pen hit reply and typed:

> Try your birthday as the combination.

"Hey, that's not bad. I use my birthday for my locker."

"I know."

Quin groaned. "So you were the one stealing pens and books from my locker last year?"

Pen didn't respond. She clicked on the second email.

> My mom wants me to take piano lessons after school, but I want to learn karate. Can you help?

She slapped her forehead. "These aren't mysteries. It's

an advice column."

Quin jumped up and leaned over the keyboard. "Allow me." He typed:

Bargain with her. Offer to take piano this semester if she'll let you do karate the next.

His twin scanned the answer. "That's pretty smart, but this isn't what I had in mind when I created SPYder."

"We're not in Abuelito's museum full of old artifacts. The mysteries around St. Mary's are—"

"Boring." Pen let the arrow hover over the last email. "If this one is about lockers or lunches or the school dance..." she muttered in a threatening tone. Quin couldn't help smiling. He felt so relieved Pen's big idea had become an advice column, he was even beginning to enjoy the questions. She clicked on the last email.

My family is in trouble and I don't know what to do. Can you help?

Both twins gasped. "Is this for real?" Quin asked.

Pen's fingers flew across the keyboard.

Let's meet on the front steps after school tomorrow.

Quin frowned as his sister hit send. "Are you sure we should be doing this? This sounds serious."

"I know. It's exactly what we hoped for."

This was nothing like he'd hoped for. Quin preferred the locker combos and piano lessons. "Who do you think it is?"

Pen closed the laptop. "I guess we'll find out tomorrow."

Quin rubbed his arm where the cast had been all summer and thought hard. Then he snapped his fingers. He had her. "If we meet whoever sent this message, they'll know we were behind SPYder. What if they tell Sister Doris?"

Pen frowned and chewed a strand of hair while returning to her search on spies in the Revolution. "We'll just have to think on our feet. Investigators have to do that all the time. We can too."

Quin stuck his hands in his pockets and slouched. "I'm glad you're finally doing some homework," he grumbled, heading to his room via their shared bathroom. He'd hoped to stay out of trouble after the mystery of the painted book, but it looked like that wouldn't be the case.

5

School dragged by the next day. Quin couldn't focus on Mr. Hardy's words. His thoughts kept leaping to the new client they were supposed to meet after school. Who would it be? What problem would they need to solve? Whatever it was, it surely wouldn't involve anything as dangerous as their last mystery, would it?

His thoughts strayed to the Friendship Cup and whether he'd be ready to play, and then to the stolen trophy. Since the theft, no new details had been uncovered and Luca had refused all interviews from the press, adding to the intrigue. Every time Quin checked his phone, new articles appeared speculating on the whereabouts of the trophy and the thief's identity. Some even thought Luca had allowed the golden ball to be stolen to create a stir around his name. As if the best player in the world needed more fame.

"Quintus Grey Reyes," Mr. Hardy called out. "Have you found a group yet?"

Quin blinked and stared down at his notebook. He'd been doodling all morning. Soccer balls, the Ballon d'Or, and a diving keeper decorated his pages.

"He's with me." Michael gave Quin a thumbs up from the next row of desks.

Quin nodded, although this meant he'd probably end up

doing most of the work.

"Great." Mr. Hardy made a note in his grade book. "And your third group member?"

"Um…" Quin had no idea what groups had already formed. Anna Callahan sat in front of Quin, her hair neatly braided and hanging down her back. She raised her hand.

"I'll join their group."

Quin and Michael exchanged a look. Michael shrugged. "Cool with me."

"Wonderful," Mr. Hardy declared. In the first two days of class, Mr. Hardy had exhibited mass amounts of enthusiasm for everything from prime numbers to classifying species of animals. It was exhausting to listen to him sometimes.

Anna twisted in her seat and beamed at Quin. He wasn't sure what he'd done to deserve it, but he smiled back and made a mental note to ask her what exactly the group assignment was.

"I wish this day would end." Michael let out a low groan. "I can't wait to play Hillside after school."

Quin nodded. He'd been looking forward to the scrimmage with Hillside Preparatory until yesterday when Pen set up the meeting with their first client. His legs danced a nervous jig beneath his desk. It's nothing, Quin told himself. Just some fifth grader with a bully problem. But the words in the text came back to him.

My family's in trouble. Can you help?

Michael punched Quin in the shoulder.

"Ow!" His best friend never realized how hard he hit. Just like Pen.

"Stop worrying. You'll be as good as Sal Cienfuegos today. Like always."

Quin nodded. If Cienfuegos handled everything coming at him with strength and skill, Quin could handle some small problem dug up by SPYder.

After school, Pen hurried to her locker to stash her books. Quin met her there, looking like he was about to lose the tasteless tacos they'd eaten in the cafeteria at lunchtime. He had his goalkeeper gloves on and bounced a soccer ball up and down. She grabbed the ball as it bounced up. "Let's go meet our client."

When they stepped outside of St. Mary's front door, a girl sat on the steps, hunched over with her arms around her knees. Pen couldn't see her face, though the afternoon sunlight highlighted the blond streaks in her hair.

The girl jumped up. Pen's eyes narrowed at Eileen Esposito. "What are you doing here?"

Eileen tucked her phone into her pocket and put her hands on her hips. "I could ask you the same thing. Shouldn't you be at that soccer scrimmage?"

Pen glowered at her. "It's a free country. That's why we had a revolution."

Eileen rolled her eyes, and nobody did it better than her, not even Pen. Pen fumed silently and squeezed the soccer ball in her hands. Why was Eileen here? Where was their client? Quin caught her eye and pointed to his watch. They had only minutes before they had to report to Coach Sikes.

"Are you meeting someone?" Eileen asked. For a moment, the hard look on her face disappeared. She looked at them questioningly.

"No, we're not waiting for anyone. Come on, Quin." Pen didn't want Eileen to even suspect they were waiting on a client. Who knew what trouble she would cause?

"But don't you want to see if—"

"No," Pen cut him off. She didn't want their client to show up now. If Eileen suspected Pen had created SPYder, she'd tell Sister Doris for sure. Eileen had held a grudge against Pen since fifth grade, when Eileen made Anna choose between being friends with her or Pen. Anna had chosen Pen and Eileen had never forgiven either of them.

Pen turned back to the steps, ready to stomp back into the school, but the door popped open and Rashelle and Darcie, two girls in Pen's class, stepped out. Darcie held a bag of jelly beans. Sister Doris never allowed this kind of contraband inside the school.

"Eileen," Darcie called out. They pushed past Pen and Quin as if the twins weren't even there. "I thought you were going to meet us inside." Darcie poured jelly beans into Eileen's hand without offering any to Pen and Quin.

Eileen shrugged. "I changed my mind." Pen frowned. Why would Eileen wait outside alone while her cronies were inside the school? Unless—oh no—the new thought made Pen stiffen.

"What?" Quin looked at Pen, his eyebrows furrowed. Pen shook her head and shoved the ball into his arms, horrified.

"What if this is a setup?" she whispered. Quin started to shake his head, then his brown eyes behind his lenses grew wide and Pen knew he understood her. What if Eileen had tried to lure SPYder's creator out to discover who it was?

"Are you sure?" he mouthed.

She shook her head. Of course she wasn't sure, but would Eileen do it? She snuck a glance at the girl. Eileen shoved a few jelly beans in her mouth and smirked at Pen. Oh yeah, Pen thought. She'd think of something this sneaky.

"Did you hear what Mariana said in class today?" Rashelle asked. "She didn't know the difference between data and date!" The girls snorted.

Pen's entire body trembled. She felt heat rush through her. When Ms. Morgan asked what kind of data they could research for their projects, Mariana had raised her hand and answered "1776." Pen made plenty of mistakes when she spoke in Spanish, not to mention Latin and Greek. It wasn't Mariana's fault *data* meant "date" in Portuguese. Still, the entire class had laughed.

"She should go back to Brazil where she belongs." Eileen's voice dripped with envy.

"*Cállate*," Pen said.

"What did you say?"

"You heard me."

"*Vamos*," Quin whispered. "*No vale la pena.*" It's not worth it.

Pen considered her brother's words and sighed. She couldn't get in trouble with the Friendship Cup coming up.

"Helloooo. I speak Spanish too." Eileen rolled her eyes. "But your brother's right, Penelope. You're not worth my time." She tossed jelly beans into her mouth and whispered to Darcie and Rashelle behind her hand.

Fury roiled in Pen, dark and stormy. "You leave Mariana da Silva alone."

"Or what?" Eileen shot back.

"Or you'll have jelly beans coming out of your nose."

Rashelle and Darcie broke into giggles and Eileen cast them a withering look. She held out her handful of jelly beans. "You just try it, Penelope, and I'll—"

Pen couldn't stand it anymore. She reached out and slapped the jellybeans from Eileen's hand. They flew through the air like colored drops of rain, scattered across the steps, and rolled into the bushes beside the school.

"Hey! What's your problem?"

"You are." Pen grabbed the soccer ball from under Quin's arm and advanced toward Eileen. Eileen's gleeful expression faltered and she scrambled up the steps to the door. "Sister Doris is still in her office."

Quin grabbed the back of Pen's shirt. "Forget it." He pulled her up the stairs. "We have better things to do."

"Like taking a shower?" Eileen called after them.

"Or brushing your hair?" Rashelle added, suddenly brave now that the twins were retreating.

Pen stiffened but Quin put both hands on her shoulders and forced her to march into the school. Pen could hardly breathe. She'd expected a client with a real problem, instead she got Eileen. She swallowed hard and blinked stinging eyes.

Quin looked at her face and said, "Take it out on Hillside."

"You bet." The venom in her voice made her brother grin.

"I already feel sorry for the other team."

They hurried to change in the locker rooms and ran down the hill to the soccer field in their blue and white uniforms. The other Saints were already warming up. Pen noted Michael and Mariana passing to each other and tried to ignore a pang of jealousy.

"Where have you two been?" Coach Sikes barked as the twins jogged to the sideline. "Never mind. Get in the goal and warm up, Quin. And you help him out, Pen."

Pen's heart sank. Usually only the younger players helped the keepers warm up.

Across the field, a team in maroon and black passed the ball back and forth with sharp precision. Hillside Preparatory was the nearest middle school and St. Mary's biggest rival. They'd beaten Hillside last spring to advance to the league final, but it'd taken a diving save by Quin to do it. Quin rubbed his right arm above the elbow, where the cast had been all summer.

"Don't worry about it," Pen said as they headed for the goal. "The doctor said your arm is stronger than ever. Maybe you should have fallen out of that tree sooner."

Her twin gave her a disdainful look and jogged to the goal. Dennis readily relinquished it to the more veteran keeper. Pen scrutinized her brother as he swung his arms wide and did a few jumps and squats. If St. Mary's were to win today, he'd have to play like the broken arm had never happened.

Pen took extra hard warm-up shots, imagining each one hitting Eileen Esposito smack in the nose. Quin didn't complain. He simply hurled the ball back to Pen with extra strength. At least one of them looked poised to do well today, she thought.

Coach Sikes called everyone together. The team grew unusually quiet as the coach scribbled on his clipboard. Finally he tugged his blue St. Mary's ball cap once and looked up.

"Here's the starting lineup. Remember, it's the first game of the season so we'll be moving some players to find out what works best for us at the tournament."

Quin exchanged a nervous look with Pen. She glanced at Dennis. Her brother had nothing to worry about. Coach Sikes would never start the scrawny fifth grader over Quin. She bit her lip and glanced at Mariana. The Brazilian stood a foot away from the others, her gaze on the far side of the field, aloof to the energy and nerves among the other players.

"I want Grey Reyes in goal." Coach Sikes looked at Quin. "Your arm feeling good?" In answer, Quin punched one gloved fist into the other hand. The coach nodded. "Good. On defense, Thompson, Jenkins, and Alvarez."

Pen nodded. These three were veteran players, no surprises there. Lyla Thompson punched Quin in the shoulder. "Don't worry, we won't even let them get a shot off." Quin rubbed his shoulder. "Thanks."

"Quiet!" Coach Sikes called. "Across the middle, let's try Vasa, Jones, Chan, and Murphy."

Not bad, Pen thought. Two starters from last year and two young, new players, but both were quick and Cal Murphy had a great left foot.

"And our two strikers..." Coach Sikes paused. "Blalock and da Silva." Pen's heart dropped to her toes and her entire body went numb. Coach Sike's voice seemed to come through a long tunnel as he talked about the substitutes staying ready to go into the game at any moment.

"Okay, Grey Reyes?" Coach Sikes asked, his voice a shade softer than normal. Pen blinked hard, pressed her lips together, and nodded. A few tear drops splattered the dust on her cleats. She swiped her hand across her face.

Pen had started every game since fifth grade, even before Quin became the starting goal keeper. It had bothered him, but Pen hadn't realized what it felt like until now. She felt so bitter she could taste it.

She glanced at Mariana. The girl had hardly reacted to being named a starter. She still stared across the field, not at the other team, but at a few spectators on the other sideline.

Coach Sikes gave last minute instructions, then they all stuck their hands into the circle and cheered. "Go Saints, beat Mustangs." The starters jogged onto the field and the rest of the team headed for the long wooden bench.

"Don't worry, you'll be in soon," Quin whispered as he walked past Pen.

Pen jerked her head. "Watch that arm of yours." She plopped hard onto the wooden bench and crossed her arms.

$$\mathcal{Q}$$

From the first whistle, Quin knew they were in trouble. The new midfielders couldn't possess the ball. Again and again his defenders kicked the ball away as the Hillside forwards attacked. Quin saved several shots, but if the team kept playing like this, it was only a matter of time until the Mustangs scored.

Only minutes later, a speedy Hillside striker juked Lyla Thompson with a dazzling move and shot the ball. Quin leaped high, but it flew past his fingers into the net. The Mustangs cheered and clapped their forward on the back.

"Come on!" Quin tossed the ball out of the net. "Get it together." They started again. This time, Michael and Mariana managed to attack the goal, but the goalkeeper stretched out to save Mariana's shot. When the first half ended, the scoreboard read 1–0. The team walked off the field with their heads down. They all knew they hadn't played their best.

Coach Sikes agreed. At halftime, he talked about

teamwork and unity and helping your teammate out while the starters stared at their feet and the substitutes nodded. Then he changed the lineup. Quin stayed in the goal, but this time Pen would play up front with Mariana.

"*Vamos Santos!*" Pen shouted, slipping into Spanish like she sometimes did on the field. "Let's do this."

From the first whistle, Pen chased every ball the Saints played up front. She dribbled at the defenders and took shots, but the Mustang goalkeeper fielded every shot. Coach Sikes subbed Michael in and Mariana took a seat on the bench. Pen exchanged thumbs ups with Michael, something they always did. "Let's go, you two!" Quin shouted.

Almost immediately Michael fielded a pass down the right sideline. He dribbled to the goal box and looked up. Pen came flying into the box and Michael sent a hard pass her way. Pen blasted it past a diving keeper into the back of the net.

Quin leaped up and shouted from his own goal. Pen high-fived Michael and her teammates.

"Let's get another one!" Lyla Thompson yelled from her position as central defender.

The game intensified, with both teams running hard and creating scoring opportunities. Quin's arm didn't hurt at all and he felt unstoppable. Was this how Salvatore Cienfuegos felt when he played for Valencia? But then a Mustang midfielder launched a pass between Thompson and Jenkins. Quin ran out to scoop up the ball, but the same speedy striker came out of nowhere and tapped the ball neatly past Quin into the goal.

Quin shouted and pounded his forehead. Why had he been thinking about Salvatore Cienfuegos and not the game? He threw the ball out of the goal toward center field, disgusted with himself. Coach Sikes made some substitutions. He called Michael off and sent Mariana up front with Pen.

There had to be only minutes left in the game. Pen kicked off to Mariana. The Brazilian passed it back to

Sanjay Vasa, who sent it to Taylor Jenkins. The Saints worked the ball around the midfield. Sanjay passed to Cal Murphy. Cal dribbled down the left wing, blowing by his defender. Pen sprinted for the goal box. Mariana ran for the far goal post. Quin held his breath and watched the play unfold. This might be their last chance to score.

Pen adjusted her run to the near post. Cal cut inside his defender and sent a cross into the box. The ball soared over Pen's head and over the goalkeeper's outstretched arms. The only one tall enough to head it in was Mariana da Silva. The Brazilian girl started to jump, then hesitated. The ball whizzed over her head and out of bounds. The ref blew the whistle and the game was over.

Quin put both gloved hands on his forehead. He couldn't believe they'd lost to Hillside. Then he heard his sister shouting. He sprinted from his goal to the other end of the field.

"What were you doing?" Pen screamed. She stormed over the Mariana. "Why didn't you head it in? You were right there."

Mariana opened her mouth and shook her head. "I—I don't know, I just..."

"We could have won. Some striker you are. I can't believe you started over me."

Quin jogged up and tugged her arm. "Come on. Let's go shake hands."

"But she should have scored," his sister protested. "It was a perfect ball. She's the only one who could have headed it in. All she had to do was—"

"I know," Quin muttered.

Michael joined them. "What's going on?"

"Nothing," Pen snapped. "Absolutely nothing to see here."

Mariana bit her lip and walked away from them, her head down.

"Lighten up, Grey Reyes," Michael said. "Headers are tough."

Pen whirled on him. "We lost the game."

Michael put his hands up. "You're right. She should have headed it." He jogged back to midfield with the rest of the team.

"You know I'm right."

Quin sighed. "Yeah. But even the best strikers miss sometimes. Even Luca."

His twin glowered at him. "So much for our Brazilian wonder." She sighed and kicked a piece of turf. "Fine, let's go shake hands."

Quin followed his sister and exchanged handshakes with the other team, hardly looking at their exuberant faces.

"Nice game," the Mustang goalkeeper told him. "Heard you broke your arm. Couldn't tell."

"Thanks. Get you next time."

"Yeah, right," the keeper laughed. "See you."

When Quin turned back, Pen gave him a murderous look. "Joking with the enemy?"

"He—" Quin started to say, then stopped. "Hey, isn't that the same man we saw watching practice last week?"

Mariana hurried across the field to a man dressed in jeans and a dark black shirt and jacket. Sunglasses and a black cap masked his identity.

Pen examined the man briefly and shrugged. "Who cares? Let's hope she never comes back."

Mariana shouted something at the man, causing a few of the Hillside parents to turn and look their way. She waved her arms as if shooing away an animal.

"What's going on?" Quin said.

"Let's go see." Pen ran toward Mariana and Quin followed.

"He's not here!" Mariana shouted. "Go away. Leave us alone."

The man reached out and grabbed Mariana's arm and spoke so low the twins couldn't hear his words, only an indistinct growl.

"Hey!" Quin ran faster. The man's eyes flicked toward them but he didn't let go of Mariana.

"Let go of her," Pen screamed.

"We're calling the police," Quin added. He realized as he said it he didn't have his phone. He'd left it in his soccer bag.

The man leaned close to Mariana and whispered something to her. Then he released her and turned away, walking quickly down the road just as the twins reached the Brazilian girl.

"Are you okay?" Pen asked. Mariana turned to them, eyes wide and face drained of color.

"Who was that?" Quin asked. "We need to call the police."

"No," the Brazilian girl snapped. "*Está bem.* I'm fine. No police." She hugged her arms around her chest and stared down the road, but the man had disappeared.

"I don't think we have a choice," Quin said. "He looked like he was about to kidnap you."

"And we saw him here last week," Pen added. "The same day you came to practice. Was he watching you?"

"*Por favor,*" Mariana pleaded. "Do not tell. He is no one." She glanced around the soccer field. "What is he doing here?"

Most of the Saints had returned to the locker rooms. Quin suddenly felt exposed. He looked around too, the hair on his neck rising. Only a few people lingered. Coach Sikes was talking to the other coach. A few parents chatted on the sideline. On the hillside, another man stared down at them. He wore a blue Boston Red Sox hat, the red B visible from across the field.

"Do you know him?" Pen asked.

"Pen, Quin, Mariana, let's go," Coach Sikes called. They glanced over at their coach. He waved them across the field. "Post-game team meeting."

When Pen and Quin turned back to the hill, the man had disappeared.

"*Isso é impossível,*" Mariana whispered.

"What? What's impossible?" Quin asked, thankful some Portuguese sounded like Spanish. He pointed to where the man in the Red Sox cap had been. "Who was that?"

Mariana bit her lip and shook her head.

"Why did that man grab you?" Pen asked. "Are you in danger?"

"It's nothing," Mariana said. "Forget these men. And you are right, Pen. I should have scored the goal."

Pen nodded slowly. "Yeah, well, sorry about my attitude. I don't like losing."

Mariana jogged away from them to the locker room.

"What was all that about?" Quin whispered.

"I don't know, but I think we better find out."

6

Mariana didn't come to school the next day.

"Maybe she's embarrassed about missing that goal yesterday," Michael suggested at lunch.

"I've seen you miss plenty of goals and you keep showing up," Quin said. Anna giggled into her chocolate milk, but Pen met Quin's eyes and both knew what their twin was thinking. Was Mariana absent because of what happened after the game?

In class, Ms. Morgan reminded her students they had one more day to turn in their topics for their projects on the American Revolution. History and algebra couldn't hold Pen's attention. She gazed out the window at the cars traveling down the street, but her mind replayed the events of yesterday. The man grabbing Mariana's arm. The Brazilian girl's plea to not call the police. She thought back to the first day they'd seen Mariana, and the stranger watching practice that afternoon. Had it been the same man who grabbed Mariana? Both wore black. It was possible. And what about the man on the hill in the Red Sox hat?

"Penelope Grey Reyes, come back to us," Ms. Morgan sang out. "We still have a few minutes of class left. And please stay after the bell."

"Ooo," the class gave a collective gasp. Eileen leaned over and whispered something to Darcie. The girls stifled laughter.

Pen tried to listen as Ms. Morgan assigned math homework and took questions on the American Revolution projects. Pen had read a half dozen accounts of spy networks on the internet, but she hadn't decided which one to focus on yet: Benjamin Franklin, Nathan Hale, or the Culper Spy Ring. Feet tapped on the tile floor and students shifted in anticipation of the bell. When it finally rang, the room emptied quickly. Ms. Morgan cleaned the whiteboard while Pen slowly made her way to the front of the classroom, her stomach all jittery. Ms. Morgan surprised her when she gave Pen a bright smile.

"I asked you to stay late because I wondered if you know where Mariana lives? I'd hate for her to fall behind in her work."

"Oh," Pen said, relief rushing through her. She didn't know, but it occurred to her this was the perfect excuse to see if Mariana was okay, or if she'd had more trouble with that man in black after yesterday.

"Actually, yes."

"Wonderful." Ms. Morgan handed her a note with the homework assignments and the written work from the school day. "And I have a favor to ask of you."

A favor from a teacher? Pen had never heard of such a thing.

"I know I said we weren't doing group projects, but I thought you and Mariana might work together on your American Revolution projects since Mariana just moved to the country."

Pen blinked at Ms. Morgan. She wanted to make sure Mariana was okay, but she didn't want to be best friends. Pen already had a best friend in Anna, plus Quin and Michael. She didn't need any more.

"Well," Pen hedged. "I don't know if Mariana will be interested in my idea."

"What is it? I notice you didn't volunteer any information in class." Ms. Morgan tilted her head and her brown eyes sparkled.

"It's a secret." Pen hated to disappoint all her enthusiasm by admitting she hadn't quite decided yet.

"Then I'm sure Mariana will love it. She seems a little secretive to me." For the first time, a shadow crossed over her teacher's bright expression.

Pen wondered if the teacher knew something she didn't. Ms. Morgan shook her head and returned to her usual self. "Shouldn't you be on your way to soccer practice?"

Pen tucked Mariana's assignments into her math book and rushed to the door.

"Thank you, Penelope," Ms. Morgan called after her.

"It's just Pen," she called back.

After practice, Pen informed her brother of her plan to drop off Mariana's homework and possibly do a little investigating in the process. Quin mulled it over. He hadn't kept his thoughts off the strange man from yesterday, the one dressed all in black on a warm September afternoon. They headed from the locker rooms, down St. Mary's empty halls to the front office. Pen planned on getting Mariana's address there.

"She's probably sick, or embarrassed at the way the game ended. Maybe she doesn't want to play on the team anymore." Quin had his soccer ball in his hands. He bounced it down the empty hallway, enjoying the echoing thumps.

Pen looked hopeful for a moment, then shook her head. "I don't think so. Remember the message on SPYder? My family's in trouble? Maybe Mariana sent it. Maybe she decided not to meet us yesterday because she's scared."

"Maybe she decided to get to the game on time so she could start." Quin immediately wished he hadn't said those words. Pen's eyes shot daggers at him.

In the office, the secretary agreed to give them the street

address once they explained about the homework. Quin cast a look at Sister Doris's closed office door. He hoped it stayed that way.

As he finished this thought, the heavy door swung open. "Ah-ha." The principal swept into the room, filling it up with her boisterous voice and black habit. She was the only sister at St. Mary's who still wore the traditional garb. The black veil mostly covered her head, but a crown of white hair poked out. Archie always joked Sister Doris would out-live every student that ever walked St. Mary's halls.

"I thought I heard your voices. What are you up to, Penelope and Quintus?"

Quin flushed. It didn't matter whether he was up to anything or not. Sister Doris always made him feel guilty.

"We're taking Mariana her homework assignments." Pen took the slip of paper the secretary offered her. Quin stared at his shoes and absentmindedly bounced the ball. Sister Doris cleared her throat and he caught the ball and pressed it to his chest to keep from bouncing it again.

"That's charitable of you." She eyed them like she didn't quite believe it. Quin offered a small smile.

"We better go. Mamá will wonder where we are." Pen shot him a look that said, 'Let's get out of here.'

Quin's phone buzzed in his pocket. He froze, well aware of Sister Doris's stance on cell phones, even though school was over for the day. The phone buzzed again.

"Just a minute," Sister Doris said. Quin's feet felt riveted to the floor. The Sister moved swiftly across the office to stand in front of him. He felt his fingers moving slowly toward his jacket pocket for the phone, even though Sister Doris hadn't asked for it.

"Let me see that soccer ball."

Quin's fingers stopped moving and clamped onto the ball. He handed it over, relieved. Then a new worry hit him. Would Sister Doris take it away for bouncing it in the office?

Sister Doris rotated the ball in her hands. He'd gotten it

for Christmas last year, a replica of a World Cup ball. Quin's mouth dropped open when Sister Doris bounced it a few times and handed it back.

"I heard we lost to Hillside yesterday. Let's not make that a habit." She nodded to both twins and returned to her office. The twins hurried to the door and burst out of the school.

"Not make it a habit?" Pen giggled.

"I thought she was going to confiscate my phone." Quin laughed, feeling like they'd somehow gotten away with something. He suddenly felt more cheerful about their trip to Mariana's. All they had to do was drop off the homework. After that maybe he could meet Michael in the park for some extra practice. "So where are we going?"

Pen consulted the paper. "It's an apartment building a few blocks away." They headed down the street. A streetcar rattled past them on its tracks, along with regular traffic. The smells wafting out of a bakery reminded Quin he hadn't eaten anything since lunch. He slowed to admire the cinnamon buns in the window.

"This is it." Pen pointed to a five-story red brick apartment building across the street. It looked old, but Quin remembered Dad saying something about the community renovating some of the older apartments. There was a break in traffic and Pen dashed across the street.

"Wait!" Of course his sister couldn't be bothered to go to the street corner and cross properly. Quin hesitated, then ran after her. His foot caught on the groove of the street car track as he stepped off the sidewalk. Quin stumbled forward, flailing to keep his balance, but he couldn't stop. He dropped the soccer ball to catch himself with his hands. The rough pavement grazed his palms and jarred his elbows and shoulders. A sharp pain shot up his newly mended arm.

"Quin!" Pen shrieked. He glanced up in time to see a dark car barreling toward him. He scrambled to his feet and tried to back away but the car was coming too fast. It was going to hit him. I knew I should have used the crosswalk, Quin thought to himself furiously, and then wondered why this was his last thought before death. Two hands clamped down on Quin's shoulders and jerked him from behind. The car raced by, missing Quin by inches. The hands released Quin and he dropped to the sidewalk in a heap. Quin gasped for breath. Every part of him trembled.

"Are you okay?" A woman kneeled beside Quin and patted his shoulder. "Should I call your parents?"

"No." Quin took a deep breath and sat up. His arms and legs still felt wobbly, like freshly baked flan. He tried to assess his injuries. Except for the quickly dulling pain in his arm and his scraped hands, he was all right.

"*Qué milagro*," he muttered.

"What's that, dear?"

"Thanks for saving me," Quin said. He looked at the woman for the first time. She was shorter than him and almost as old as Abuela. He thought of the powerful pull that yanked him out of the car's path just in time. The woman must be stronger than she looked. A hundred times stronger.

"I didn't save you." She pointed down the sidewalk. "A man did. I saw it all from the bakery." Quin stared at the man she pointed to, but he'd already crossed to the next block. All Quin could see were long legs, hands shoved into his pockets, and a blue baseball cap.

"I guess he didn't want to be thanked," the woman added. "Should we call the police? Do you have a phone? Mine is inside the bakery."

Quin got to his feet and tested his flan-like legs. They seemed to support him. Across the street, Pen waved at him, her face as pale as he'd ever seen it. He lifted his hand to wave back and winced. Maybe his arm wasn't as healed as he thought.

"I have a phone, but I don't think we need to call." Quin stuck his hand in his jacket pocket. "Hey, where is it?" He turned in a circle. "Did you see my phone?"

The woman shook her head. They examined the side-walk and street where Quin had fallen. No phone. He groaned. He'd just gotten this phone and now he'd have to tell his parents how he lost it.

"Wait here a minute." The woman disappeared into the bakery. Quin picked a few tiny stones out of his palms, wincing with each one. They left indentations in his hands but didn't bleed. He wondered what they'd feel like in practice tomorrow.

"Take these," the woman said, reappearing. "Something to take your mind off everything. And for goodness sake, use the crosswalk next time." She tucked a white bag into Quin's hands, patted his arm, and walked away. Quin walked in a daze to the street light and crossed properly. Pen met him on the other side.

"Are you okay? That was crazy."

"Yeah, *loco*." Quin swallowed hard. More like terrifying.

"What if I had to tell Mamá you got run over?" His sister shook her head. All the color had returned to her cheeks. "If that man hadn't pulled you back, you'd be—"

Pen stopped suddenly and bit her lip. Her eyes watered.

"The man who helped me, did you see him?"

She shook her head. "No. I mean I saw him, but I was watching you and that stupid soccer ball."

"My ball. Where is it?"

The twins searched up and down the street and under parked cars. They found no sign of the ball.

"It's gone." Quin sighed. "I can't believe it. I lost my phone and my soccer ball at the same time."

Pen looked at him sharply. "Your phone?" She shook her head. "Better not tell Mamá and Dad. In fact..." she scruti-nized him from head to toe. "Let's not mention any of this. Is that what you and the old lady were looking for? Maybe she took it."

Quin held up the bakery bag. "A thief who gives her vic-tims pastries?"

Pen shrugged. "Oh well, you didn't like having a phone

anyway."

Quin didn't respond that he'd gotten used to having one, and being able to check the European League news any time of day had been exhilarating.

His twin tugged his arm. "Come on. What's in the bag?"

He shrugged and peered inside. The scent of cinnamon wafted out and made his mouth water. Two huge cinnamon rolls nestled inside the bag, dripping warm icing on the tissue paper.

"Oh good," Pen said, looking into the bag. "We can take them to Mariana."

"But—" Quin protested, but Pen had already disappeared inside the apartment building. He sniffed the bag again. The smell of the rolls made his stomach grumble. It was good to be alive, Quin reflected.

Pen knocked hard on the door of the third-floor apartment. They waited in the hall for several long minutes while the cinnamon rolls cooled. Quin stuck his finger in the bag and swiped some frosting off the top. As he licked his fingers, he realized he'd skinned his knuckles in his fall. He grabbed a napkin from the bag and pressed it against the scrapes.

"Maybe no one's home. You could leave the homework outside the door."

Pen frowned and double checked the address. "But we still wouldn't know if Mariana is okay or not."

A lock slid open on the other side of the door and it cracked open. "Who is it?" a man called roughly, his accent thicker than Mariana's.

"Pen and Quin Grey Reyes. We're friends of Mariana's." Pen answered the man with her usual boldness. Quin took a step back, not liking the man's tone.

"She's not here." The door slammed shut.

"But we have her homework," Pen told the closed door. Voices echoed inside the apartment, the man's and a higher-pitched voice, arguing in Portuguese. Then the door jerked open.

Mariana stood in front of them, her cheeks flushed and her green eyes flashing. *"Desculpe,"* she apologized. *"Meu pai*, my father, he—"

The voice behind her mumbled indistinctly. Mariana glanced over her shoulder and brushed a strand of hair behind her ear.

"Are you okay?" Pen whispered.

Mariana nodded. *"Claro.* I did not feel well today. You have my homework?"

Pen shoved the stack of papers at the girl. Quin stepped forward and handed her the bag of cinnamon rolls as well.

Mariana looked surprised but took them.

"I guess we'll see you tomorrow?" Pen asked.

Mariana hesitated, then leaned forward and whispered. *"Sim.* We must talk."

"Mariana, shut the door," Mariana's father said in Portuguese.

Mariana shot the twins a wide-eyed look. "Tomorrow." She banged the door shut.

The twins turned away and clumped down the stairwell. Pen shook her head. "She was scared."

"I'd be scared of her dad, too." Quin's stomach growled. Why hadn't he taken one cinnamon roll? Mariana wouldn't have known how many had been in the bag.

"It's more than that," his twin said as they reached the first floor and headed for the door. "When he first opened the door, did you see how he looked at us?"

"Like he thought we were going to force our way in?"

"Exactamente."

They walked out to the sidewalk. "Hey, my ball." Quin spied his soccer ball under the bushes lining the sidewalk. He grabbed it and moaned. "It's flat. A car probably hit it."

"Better than hitting you. What's this?" Pen pointed to a small tear in the leather skin

Quin groaned. "Oh no. It's useless."

"I meant what's inside the hole?"

A piece of paper poked out of it. He grasped the paper and pulled. A small note slid out. He paused and examined the tear closely. "This is strange. If a car hit it, the ball should be busted." He ran his finger along the tear. "This is so small, it's almost like someone slit it open with a knife?"

He turned to Pen, confused. She grabbed the note from his hand, opened it, and gasped. Quin pulled it from her hand and read out loud.

"Stay away from Mariana and her family or you'll lose more than a soccer ball."

7

Mariana hardly spoke to Pen at school the next day. Even though they sat next to each other, she kept her eyes on Ms. Morgan and ignored Pen's whispered attempts to talk. Pen wrote her two notes to ask if she was okay and tell Mariana about their project proposal, which was due at the end of class. After Mariana threw both notes Pen tossed on her desk back without opening them, Ms. Morgan finally stopped teaching and gave Pen a stern look.

"Is there something you need to tell the class, Penelope?"

Pen stashed the notes inside her history book and shook her head, frustrated. Not only could she not ask Mariana about the note they'd found in Quin's ball, but they hadn't discussed their American Revolution project, either.

Pen glared at Mariana's blond hair, but the Brazilian girl wouldn't look at her. Why had she said they needed to talk yesterday and now wouldn't even look at Pen?

The only bright spot in Pen's day was when she turned in her project proposal, which she'd reluctantly added Mariana's name to. She'd chosen to research the secret ways spies communicated during the American Revolution by focusing on the Culper Spy Ring. Ms. Morgan's eyes lit up when she read the brief paragraph. "This looks intriguing. I can't wait to see what you and Mariana learn."

Pen nodded, surprised she felt the same way.

In practice, she missed several easy goals and Coach Sikes yelled at her to get her head in the game, even though it was only a team scrimmage. Mariana scored three goals, each more perfect than the other. By the time practice ended, Pen was fuming. She stalked toward Mariana, ready to confront the girl, but Coach Sikes stepped in front of her.

"I want you to take some extra shooting practice with your brother and some of the midfielders."

"But Coach, I—"

Coach Sikes tugged on his blue Saints cap and frowned. "You don't think you need extra practice?"

Pen wilted. She'd been awful today and she knew it. "Okay," she whispered, watching Mariana jog up the stairs two at a time and disappear into the locker rooms.

Thirty minutes later, Coach Sikes blew his whistle to end the extra practice. Pen jogged toward the locker room, exhausted but feeling a little better. She'd landed nearly every shot. She hadn't realized the pressure she felt to play better when Mariana was around.

Quin caught up to her at the top of the stairs, breathing hard from the climb. "Way to go," he muttered. "My arm's killing me."

"Thanks." She recognized the hidden compliment. "Did Mariana talk to you today?"

Quin slapped his goalkeeper gloves into his palm and shook his head. "Not a word. She didn't even thank me for the cinnamon rolls."

Pen sighed. "She wouldn't even say hi today. What's with this girl?"

He shrugged as they headed to their separate locker rooms. "Maybe she changed her mind. After the way you played today, we should worry about the Friendship Cup."

"I am," Pen muttered. She split off from Quin to enter the girls' locker room and grab her gear before heading to the bus stop in front of St. Mary's. When she came out, she almost ran right into a man taking the trash out of a can near the entryway. long hair disheveled.

"Oh, sorry. I didn't see you," she said. She recognized the man dressed in jeans and a light blue St. Mary's T-shirt as the new janitor Sister Doris had introduced at the school assembly. The man glared at her and grunted.

"It's not like I meant to," Pen muttered under her breath as she passed him.

Quin came out of the boys room. "What?"

She glanced back over her shoulder. Something about the janitor seemed familiar, but she wasn't sure why. He'd already entered the boys' locker room. Pen shrugged. "Nothing. Let's go home."

Together the twins jogged across the empty gym, down the main hall, and out the front door.

Late afternoon traffic buzzed by. This close to rush hour, the bus would be late. Pen plopped onto a bench to wait. So many problems whirled through her head, she didn't know which to settle on first. Mariana stealing her position. The man tugging Mariana away after the scrimmage. The way Mariana's father acted yesterday and the Brazilian girl's whispered 'we need to talk.' Not to mention her refusal to even look at Pen today. And then the note in Quin's ball. Who left it? Why did they need to stay away from Mariana?

Quin sat silently beside her. He'd borrowed her phone to check the mid-week soccer updates. "Who do you think took it?" he muttered.

"Took what?"

"Luca's trophy," Quin said. "The golden ball. It says here they don't have any leads on who stole it."

Pen had nearly forgotten about the missing trophy with everything else happening. "I don't know. What can we do about it?"

The phone buzzed and Pen lunged to grab it. Quin pulled it away and glanced at the screen.

"Why's Michael texting you?"

"None of your business." Pen stood up and grabbed the phone. "Last time I loan this to you."

She checked the text. It was from Michael. Her stomach fluttered a little.

What's up 2day? U missed like 4 goals.

Pen quickly dashed off a text to Michael.

Even Luca has off days. I'll do better tomorrow.

She almost added 'What's up with you and Mariana?' but didn't. Michael and Mariana had played well together today. Part of Pen's frustration stemmed from this fact. No one else had sent an inquiry through SPYder, either. No follow-ups to the mysterious *my family is in trouble* text. Whose family? Why hadn't their client come forward? Pen had even sent a follow-up text suggesting another meeting and gotten no response.

And on top of all that, Eileen Esposito had smiled at Pen every chance she got today—a smile that said, 'I'm on to you, Penelope.' Pen wondered when Eileen would go to Sister Doris and tell her she suspected Pen was behind SPYder. She told her brother about Eileen and SPYder while they waited.

"Maybe we should do what the note said and stay away from Mariana for now," Quin said.

Pen glowered at the traffic, her face as sultry as the warm afternoon. "Fine," she snapped.

"*Ssssss.*"

Pen cocked her head. "Did you hear something?"

"Somebody's tire," Quin muttered.

"*Sssssssss,*" it came again. A hand waved at them from the shadows of a café door down the street from the school. The wrist had a slim silver bracelet on it and the nails were perfectly manicured and painted pale pink. Pen had seen those hands before.

"Mariana?" Pen stood up and took a step toward the café.

"Where?" Quin stood too.

The bus rumbled down the street and squealed to a

stop. Mariana darted from the café door to the bus and jumped aboard. Quin shrugged at Pen and they followed her on the bus. They found Mariana slumped in a seat at the back.

"*Olá,*" she said quietly. The bus jerked into motion and Pen sat next to Mariana with Quin across the aisle.

"*Hola*?" Pen said. "That's all you can say? You ignored me all day and you say *hola*? I had to turn in our project proposal without getting to talk to you. We're doing the Culper Spy Ring, by the way."

"I'm sorry," Mariana whispered. "I couldn't talk at school. *Minha família...*" She stopped and chewed on her nails.

Pen forgot her frustration immediately, her curiosity getting the best of her. What's wrong?" Mariana was acting like a spy who'd blown her cover. "Are you in trouble? Is someone following you?"

"Why would you say that?" Mariana cried out. She looked around them. The other passengers were busy scanning their phones or looking out the window. A toddler smiled and waved at them from a few rows away, the only person paying any attention to them. Still, Mariana leaned in and whispered.

"Can we go someplace to talk? Maybe, *sua casa*?"

Quin shrugged. "Our parents won't be home for at least another hour."

"If that," Pen added. Sometimes their parents got so absorbed in their work, they came home late.

The bus screeched up to another stop and all three had to brace against the seats. "What do your parents do?"

"Dad works for a tech company; Mom's a professor and archaeologist," Quin answered.

"Cool," Mariana said. "My mom cleans houses. In Brazil she was a teacher."

"And your dad?" Pen remembered their encounter with the man last night.

Mariana frowned and shook her head. "I don't want to

talk about it here."

The bus ground to the top of the hill, affording a magnificent view of the Boston skyline and harbor. Pen ignored it. Everything about the way Mariana acted pointed to a mystery. She couldn't wait to get to the house and talk. Mariana followed the twins out the back door of the bus. Pen coughed and waved at the exhaust as the bus pulled away.

They cut across the neighborhood park and trudged up the hill, sweating in their soccer shorts and Saints T-shirts. Mariana had changed from her Saints practice gear and wore heeled sandals, a yellow skirt, and a white tank top and didn't seem to sweat a drop. Pen shook her head. Maybe she was used to the heat. Wasn't Brazil hot most of the year? It wasn't a country Kostas had the twins study in their summer lessons with the Greek tutor.

They headed to the back of the house and dropped their school bags in the mudroom. The house was silent, except for the occasional pop as the old ceilings and wooden floorboards expanded with the heat of the day. Mariana took in the Grey Reyes home with one lifted eyebrow while Quin grabbed some apples for a snack.

Pen led the way through the dining room to the entry hall and a sweeping wooden staircase. They thumped and creaked their way up the old wooden steps, which dated from the late nineteenth century. Pen and Quin's rooms were on the same side of the hall, separated by their shared bathroom. Archie's room and a guest room graced the other side, though Archie only occupied his room on weekends he came home from his dorm room at MIT.

Pen shoved dirty clothes off her bed and kicked them underneath. Quin walked to the window and opened the shade to let in sunlight, even though Pen glared at him. Mariana examined several laptops cluttering Pen's desk. One she used. The others she and Archie were stripping for parts.

"Computers and a *futebol* star. You are talented,"

Mariana murmured.

"Um, thanks." Mariana thought she was a soccer star? Quin tossed an apple to Mariana while giving Pen a look that said, 'See, she's not so bad.' She almost stuck her tongue out, but Mariana looked over, so she bit it instead.

"Ouch, I mean, what did you want to talk about?" She rubbed her tongue against the roof of her mouth and plopped onto her unmade bed.

Mariana scratched her arm, her gaze roaming around the messy room.

"Sit here," Quin suggested, removing an old hard drive from the desk chair and pulling it out for Mariana.

"*Obrigada,*" Mariana said. "And thank you for the cinnamon buns yesterday." She gave Quin a shy smile. Quin smiled back. He backed up to the foot of Pen's bed, sat down, and yelped.

"Ow, what is this?" Quin searched beneath the covers and produced the culprits, a pair of needle-nose pliers and a tiny screwdriver.

"You found them. Archie was mad at me for los—I mean, misplacing them." Pen took the tools from Quin and laid them on her night stand. Then she gave Mariana her full attention. "So what's going on?"

Pen ignored Quin's frown. He always chastised her for jumping straight into a matter, but why waste time?

Mariana bit into her apple and chewed slowly. Pen fidgeted. "Oh tell us already," she finally burst out. "Mamá and Dad will be home soon."

Mariana carefully set the half-eaten apple on Pen's desk and daintily licked the juice from her fingers. Geez, Pen thought. She looked like a model even while being sloppy.

"*Bom,*" Mariana said. "I said I would talk so I will. It's just..." she lowered her voice. "I do not know who to trust." She hugged her bare arms across her chest.

Pen and Quin exchanged a quick glance and nodded. "Mariana," Quin said, his voice almost as quiet as hers, "Pen and I have experience with..." He paused and Pen saw he was struggling for an explanation. How do you tell a stranger about getting entwined in a search for a centuries-old Mexican painted book, only to have it nearly end with your death?

"With international intrigue," Pen stepped in.

Mariana hesitated, then nodded. "I know you want to help. That's why I wanted to talk to you."

"But how did you know it was us behind SPYder?" Pen asked.

"What do you mean? I asked for help because of what you said in class the other day. You asked Ms. Morgan if someone had an emergency, shouldn't they ask for help? And then you came to help me after the game when—" she stopped and rubbed her arms again, even though the bedroom was still warm in the sunlight.

"So you didn't text SPYder that you needed help? Or that your family was in trouble?"

Mariana shook her head.

en fumed silently. Then Eileen Esposito had masqueraded as a client the other day, probably hoping to catch Pen admitting she was SPYder. Pen would show her not to mess with an international agent of intrigue.

"What was going on the other day at the soccer game? And yesterday with your dad?" Quin asked, bringing Pen back to the present problem.

Pen immediately recognized the look on Mariana's face. It brought back vivid memories from the summer and being held hostage by a crazy, gun-wielding art student. Mariana was afraid. She bit her lip and shook her head. "I cannot tell you. It's too dangerous."

"Then why are you here?" Pen knew her outburst sounded rude. But was Mariana just playing games with them? And part of her was still thinking about Eileen Esposito and trying to devise an appropriate plan of revenge.

"Whatever it is, you can trust us," Quin hurried to say.

Mariana nodded. "*Bom,*" she whispered. "You are right. I must trust someone." Her face shifted to the resoluteness she displayed on the soccer field. "My last name is da Silva."

"Right," Quin said. "Like Luca da Silva. Not that you're related."

"Da Silva is one of the most common names in Brazil," Mariana said. "Many people have this name but are not related to Luca." She stopped rubbing her arms and dropped them to her sides. "But I am. Luca is my uncle."

Quin shot off the bed. "That's impossible. No, incredible, it's..." He clutched his head and spun around.

"He's my father's younger brother, but he's more like my brother, not my uncle."

Quin stopped spinning. "You grew up with Luca? Did you play soccer with him?"

Mariana shrugged. "Of course."

Quin flopped onto his back on Pen's bed and rubbed his eyes. "Impossible," he whispered.

"Get a hold of yourself." Pen socked her twin in the arm. Not the one he'd broken. She wasn't that cruel. "No wonder you don't tell people if they all act like this."

Quin rubbed his arm and sat on the edge of the bed. "Amazing," he whispered.

"*Está tudo bem,* it's fine. Everyone in my school at home knew. They treated me like I was the star."

Pen snorted softly. No wonder this girl expected everyone on the soccer field to worship her. Her hopes for an international mystery had fallen away. It sounded like Mariana just missed being Luca's famous niece. "So, you want us to tell other people you're related to Luca?"

"No." Mariana sounded horrified.

"Okaaay." Pen got off her bed and wandered to the window, restless. She'd had enough of this prima donna. The voice of Kostas, their jolly Greek tutor, popped into her head.

"What's the Latin form of the word, Penelope?" Kostas would ask.

"*Prima domina.* First lady," Pen whispered, staring out

her window. Sunlight slanted across the two slim maple trees in the backyard they used for goalposts.

"So how can we help?" Quin finally asked. He sounded more than happy to help. Of course he did. Mariana was related to Luca, the best soccer player in the world. Pen sighed and turned back to Mariana.

"Have you ever heard of the Ballon d'Or?" Mariana asked.

"Are you serious? The golden ball?" Quin said. "It's the trophy given to the best footballer of the year. Your uncle won it in January. He's the youngest player to ever win it, and in his first season. And somebody stole it."

"*Correto*," Mariana chimed in Portuguese. She gave Quin a brief smile. Pen frowned and wished the girl would quit speaking Portuguese. It only made her sound more exotic.

"I'm sorry about all of that," Pen said. "But what can we do about it?"

Mariana drew her long legs up and hugged her knees to her chest. "I want you to help me find my uncle's trophy. She looked up and her green eyes glistened fiercely. "Help me find out who stole the Ballon d'Or."

8

"Why are you asking us to help you find the golden ball? Shouldn't that be a job for the police?" Quin's question hung in the air.

Pen's heart thumped in her chest. She couldn't believe it. When she created SPYder, she had hoped for a mystery, but this was beyond what she'd imagined. Still, Pen couldn't help but feel a stab of jealousy and resentment. Did this girl think she could show up at St. Mary's and take Pen's spot on the team and then ask for her help?

Mariana tapped her fingers on Pen's desk, not answering them. Her eyes darted around the room. "No *policia*." The same words she used on the soccer field when the strange man in black tried to take Mariana with him. "*É perigroso*. Dangerous," she echoed in English.

Quin leaned forward from his seat on the bed. "Why? If this is about the man the other day at the game, we should tell the police—"

"No," Mariana shouted and stood up. Blood rushed to her cheeks. "You do not understand." Tears began to roll from her eyes. "My family is in trouble if the police search for the trophy. Luca, my mother, Papai." Mariana swallowed and brushed the tears away.

Pen straightened up from leaning on her desk. My family is in trouble. The same text from their client on SPYder.

Mariana had to be their client and Eileen Esposito had scared her off the day they were to meet. She felt sure of it. And relieved Eileen didn't know she was behind SPYder after all.

"Okay," Pen said. She sat down on the bed next to her twin. "Who's threatening them?" At Mariana's confused look, she added, "Why are they in danger?"

Mariana sniffed. "The man who took the trophy left Luca a note. It said if he called the police, they will hurt his family. We are the only family Luca has."

"Wow," Quin whispered, and this time his voice held none of the excitement over knowing Luca.

Pen's mind whirred like the laptop on her desk. "If they're threatening your family, does that mean they know you moved to Boston?"

Mariana rubbed her arms. Pen noticed goose bumps on them and felt her own arms prickle.

"*Eu não sei*. One day we lived in *Brasil*, the next Papai says we are moving here." Her large green eyes filled with tears. "We came here before the Ballon d'Or was stolen. But since I started school, I feel like..." Mariana stopped talking and blinked back tears.

"Like someone's following you?" Quin touched the scrapes on his knees as if thinking about yesterday's narrow escape.

"*Sim*," she whispered.

"And the man in black?" Pen asked. "The man who talked to you after the soccer game? Is he threatening you?"

Mariana hesitated. Then she shrugged and shook her head. "You must help. There is no one else."

Mariana's words broke through Pen's jealousy. Maybe Mariana was a better soccer player than she was, but it didn't mean they couldn't take the case. Then another thought struck her. If they found the trophy, maybe Mariana would move back to Brazil and Pen would be back in her spot as starting forward on the team.

Quin shook his head. "I don't know. It sounds like whoever took the trophy is dangerous. And if they're in Boston..." He didn't finish the sentence.

"Come on, *hermano*," Pen encouraged. "We can do this." Suddenly, the thrill of a new mystery filled her and she felt as excited as she did at the start of a game.

Her twin frowned but pushed his curly brown hair away from his glasses and cleared his throat. "I guess we can at least look a little. It *is* the Ballon d'Or."

Pen heard the hint of excitement in his voice and grinned. That was all she needed. She stood up from her desk and held out her hand to Mariana. "We'll take your case."

Half an hour later, the three were sprawled across Pen's bed, deep into researching the Ballon d'Or on the internet when Mamá knocked on the bedroom door.

"Homework already?" Mamá asked as she opened the door. "*Que estudiosos*! And who's this? *Una nueva amiga*?"

"Mamá," Pen groaned. She shut the laptop so her mother couldn't see they weren't studying.

Mariana stood up from where she sat on Pen's bed. "*É tarde*. My mother will worry I'm so late."

"You're the new Brazilian girl *mis hijos* have talked so much about. What a nice surprise." She shot the twins a puzzled look. Pen knew it was because she hadn't said one nice thing about Mariana at home, especially after losing the game.

"*Sim*, but I should go." She hesitated and looked at both twins, obviously not wanting to say more.

Pen gave an almost imperceptible shake of her head. "See you tomorrow at school."

Mariana nodded. "*Bom*. See you." She gave Maria Grey Reyes a hesitant smile and slipped past her to the stairs.

"Aren't you going to walk your friend out?" Mamá demanded. It wasn't a question.

Quin jumped up. "I'll do it." Quin hurried to catch Mariana. Pen could hear muffled voices at the front door.

"I'm so pleased to see you taking your school work seriously," Mamá told Pen. "As soon as you finish your homework, come down to the kitchen and help me with the *ensalada*."

As soon as her mother left, Pen grabbed her phone. She wanted to help Mariana find the golden ball, but all her international agent instincts told her the girl was hiding something, too. She chewed her lip. The problem with Luca being a world-famous soccer player was almost anyone could be a suspect for stealing the trophy. How could they figure out who it was and who was threatening Mariana's family? She needed help from someone who knew how to search the web for clues and who could keep his mouth shut.

Pen needed Archie.

She opened the encrypted text program her older brother installed on her phone. When they communicated, they used code names, sort of like the revolutionary spies. Pen had been nicknamed π because it was an irrational number. When Pen protested, Archie pointed out pi was also a transcendent number. Pen decided she preferred being superior to irrational, so she relented. She typed:

π: I need help.

After a moment, Archie's code name, the Greek letter α or Alpha, popped up.

α: SPYder troubles?

π: Sort of.

α: Intrigued. Meet mañana after school. At MIT?

π: Perfecto. Thx.

"Penelope?" Mamá's voice floated up the stairs. "*La ensalada* is not making itself."

Pen sighed and pocketed the phone. They would have to wait another whole day before starting their search for the Ballon d'Or. She walked downstairs in a daze, her mind still turning over the new information Mariana had revealed. Why would someone steal a world-famous trophy and threaten Mariana and her family? Now it was her and Quin's job to find out.

$$\varphi$$

As much as Quin enjoyed Mr. Hardy's class, the school day crawled by. He couldn't concentrate on the American Revolution, even though some wonderful art had been inspired and created from that era. When Mr. Hardy asked who had ridden through the streets at midnight warning the countryside the British were coming, Quin said it was John Revere.

"Sorry, but it's Paul Revere," Mr. Hardy answered. "But I often confuse John and Paul, too." He laughed and the students looked at each other, bewildered. "Never mind." Their teacher sighed. "Let's talk about the first British invasion."

Quin tried to listen, but soon his mind meandered back to the details of Mariana's story and his stomach jumped more than a spooked horse. Pen had sworn them all to secrecy yesterday until they could meet with Archie. When he asked his twin how to keep quiet that Mariana was Luca da Silva's niece, she responded, "Just act like it's a normal day."

Easy for her to say. Delving into dangerous situations didn't seem to faze her. Quin's hands and knees still stung from his narrow miss with the car. He couldn't figure out how it all happened. The car suddenly swerving toward him, the man pulling him out of the way and then disappearing. His lost phone. The deflated soccer ball with a note warning them away from Mariana, and the most surprising thing of all: finding out the greatest soccer player in the world was Mariana's uncle.

"Act normal," Quin muttered under his breath. "Yeah right."

Anna turned around in her seat. "What'd you say?"

"Uh, nothing."

"Oh, okay." Anna waited and twirled her braid. Quin noticed the smattering of freckles across her nose and cheeks. She turned back around when he didn't say anything else, her lips pressed into a pout. Quin felt like he'd insulted her and had no idea why. He decided this school day couldn't get any longer.

After soccer practice, Coach Sikes called the team together. "Don't forget about the parent meeting tonight. If your parents don't sign the tournament permission slips, you won't be able to play." The team gathered together and ended practice the same way they always did, hands in the center and cheering, "Go Saints," on the count of three.

Quin jogged up the steps to the gym locker room and changed into a clean pair of shorts and his white Valencia jersey. Then he rubbed some water over his face and through his hair before putting his glasses on.

"Hot date?" Michael grabbed his bag from his locker, not bothering to change out of his cleats.

In the mirror, Quin's cheeks flushed. "*Cállate.* We're going to see Archie, that's all."

"At MIT? Cool. Can I come?"

Quin hesitated. Michael was his best friend, but his sister had been clear yesterday. Nobody else could know about Luca and the stolen trophy, even though Quin had been bursting all day to tell his friend everything.

"Quin," Pen shouted at the locker room entrance. "*Qué haces*? Mariana and I are ready."

Michael frowned. "Oh, I get it. Mariana's going. No wonder you're mooning at the mirror. It's too late, Grey Reyes. She saw you all sweaty and ugly at practice."

Quin balled up his practice jersey and threw it but Michael ducked. "Never mind." His best friend laughed. "I already asked her to the Fall Fest Dance. She said yes."

"You did?" Quin crammed his dirty gear into his school

bag while he tried to shift from international theft to St. Mary's first dance of the school year. "But that's not until October."

Michael shrugged. "You have to ask early or you'll be stuck dancing with Sister Doris."

Quin snorted. If Sister Doris asked you to dance, it was the kiss of death to any more invitations the rest of the night, and possibly even the school year.

"Who are you taking?" Michael ran his hands through his curly blond hair.

Quin swung his bag onto his shoulder and shrugged. "Haven't thought about it," he muttered, though a girl did pop into his head. Pen would kill him if she knew. He asked a question to get the thought out of his mind.

"Hey, does my sister know you asked Mariana?"

Michael slicked back a few out of place hairs and smiled at himself in the mirror. His blue eyes met Quin's and he raised his brows. "No. Why would she care?" He cocked his head, waiting for an answer.

"Um—"

"What are you doing in here? Getting ready for the dance?" Pen exploded into the boys' locker room. Her dark hair, still in a ponytail, swung violently and sweaty tendrils clung to her face. She hadn't changed out of her practice clothes, though she'd put on her black street soccer shoes.

"Nice, Pen, what if I'd been in the shower?" Michael gave her a half smile.

"Like you shower," she shot back. Quin shook his head. No wonder Michael had asked Mariana to the dance and not Pen.

"*Olá?*" Mariana called out. "Is it okay to come in?" She poked her head into the locker room. Her long hair hung neatly down her back and she'd changed into a green skirt and blue striped top. Her sandals had thick heels that made her tower over them.

"So can I come with you guys?" Michael repeated. He aimed the question at the twins, but he didn't take his eyes off of Mariana, so he missed Pen's scowl.

"Did you tell him?" Pen mouthed to Quin.

He returned his sister's frown and shook his head. Pen's dark look lessened and she nodded.

"That depends. How good are you at keeping secrets?"

"Secrets? The best." Michael winked at Quin.

"Fine," Pen snapped. "You can come."

Quin's mouth dropped open. She'd sworn him to secrecy all day and just like that she was going to share everything with Michael?

"*Vamos*?" Mariana said. "We have a parent meeting tonight about the Friendship Cup. If I'm not here, my mother will worry."

"Yeah, *vamos*." Michael grabbed his gym bag and reached out to take Mariana's from her shoulder. The two of them headed out of the locker room.

"You think that's a good idea?" Quin asked as he gathered his own stuff.

"No, but Michael would have badgered you until you told him where we were going."

Quin gave her a sheepish grin.

"Oh, you already did." Pen sighed. "Oh well. He might be useful. If I don't kill them both before we get there."

She hurried out of the locker room, her shoes slapping extra hard on the tile floor.

Quin wondered how long it would be before she found out about the Fall Fest dance. He knew one thing for certain. He wouldn't be the one to tell her.

They took the subway deeper into Boston and exited at the MIT stop. Mariana and Michael gaped at the two Greek columns marking the entry to campus. The twins had visited Archie before, but Pen still felt a shiver of awe as they crossed the campus and its strange mix of modern and Greek-style buildings. She popped out her smart phone and texted Archie. He replied almost immediately.

α: Meet at Barker Library. The one w/huge dome.

She redirected their route toward the large domed building. They walked across a green expanse where coeds threw Frisbees, lounged, and cast the group of middle-schoolers odd looks. A Frisbee landed nearby and Michael casually picked it up and tossed it back.

"Cool place. Maybe I'll look into it."

Pen caught her eye roll just in time. If Michael wanted to apply to college here, why should she make fun just because he'd never shown any interest in technology before? She supposed there were other things to study here, though it was the Massachusetts Institute of *Technology*.

"*É lindo*," Mariana said.

Pen nodded. Mariana was right. It was beautiful. They approached the large, white domed library that reminded her of a summer spent with Kostas exploring Greece. This building wouldn't look out of place at the Acropolis.

Archie paced back and forth beneath the colonnade. He waved when he saw them.

"This is your brother?" Mariana asked.

Pen glanced over and didn't hold the eye roll this time. She'd seen this look on other girls' faces. Even Anna, who'd grown up knowing Archie, treated him differently since he'd started at MIT.

"Yeah," Quin said, oblivious. "He graduated a year early, but don't let on if you think he's a genius. His head's already big enough."

A smile flitted across Mariana's face and her pale cheeks colored. Pen realized she wasn't the only one gauging Mariana's reaction. Michael frowned at Archie.

"Hey, four particles," Archie greeted them. "Guess that makes me the Alpha."

Michael and Mariana looked mystified. Quin shrugged at Pen. She sighed. "It's a joke. In physics, alpha particles are made up of four smaller particles. Two neutrons and two protons. So that's us." Of course, only she and Quin knew Archie's code name was Alpha, so Michael and

Mariana couldn't appreciate the humor.

"A physics joke. Awesome," Michael said in a tone that sounded less than enthused. "Is this why we came all the way out here?"

Archie laughed. "Who invited you, knucklehead? Pen said there'd be three of you. He took in Mariana for the first time. "So you're the Brazilian girl giving my siblings all kinds of fits on the soccer field."

"Archie," the twins shouted at their brother. Several students glanced at them.

"I thought we were being subtle here," Archie said. "Aren't we looking into a mystery?"

"Shh," Pen shushed him. "Let's go somewhere we can talk in private."

"A mystery?" Michael said. "Now we're talking." They hadn't been able to explain the reason for their trip to MIT to him on the subway, but Michael had spent almost the entire ride telling Mariana about his two weeks of soccer camp. Mariana didn't say much, but she did look mildly impressed. Pen had wanted to tell Michael how they solved the mystery of the painted book in Mexico, but their grandfather had made the twins promise not to mention it.

"Let's find a study room," Archie suggested. "Then you can tell me why the four of you are risking being late for a soccer meeting to talk to me. We could have video-chatted, you know."

Pen shook her head firmly. "Not for this, *hermano*."

They filed into the library's cool interior and found an empty study room on the main floor, underneath the library's dome. Then Pen and Quin told Archie about the stolen trophy.

"So just to summarize," Archie said, running both hands through his black hair until it stood up in tufts instead of its normal curls, "your world-famous uncle got his trophy stolen and won't go to the police because of a threat to his family—you." He pointed to Mariana, "And you want me to help you find the guys who stole the trophy? The same ones who are threatening your family? And you want us to do all this without talking to the police?"

Mariana cocked her head and chewed her lower lip. She gazed through the window of their private study room onto the main floor of the library. Then she nodded once. "*Sim. Exato.*"

"Your family is crazy," Michael said to Pen. "And so is this. Let's do this." He pounded the table with one fist. A librarian shelving books nearby frowned at them through the glass.

Pen slammed her hand on top of Michael's, effectively ending the distraction. "You said you could keep a secret." His hand felt warm and sweaty. She pulled her hand away.

"I can, but this isn't a regular secret. It's Luca da Silva." His voice rose again. "I mean, come on."

Quin nodded. "I know. I wanted to tell you all day."

"I can't believe you didn't."

"*Por favor,*" Mariana shouted. Someone tapped on the outside of the glass window. The same librarian frowned into their study room. The bald-headed man shook his head and brought a finger to his lips. Archie waved and mouthed "sorry." The rest tried to look penitent. The librarian gave them a dubious look before moving on.

"You four better not get my library privileges revoked," Archie muttered. He leaned back in his chair and shook his head. "That trophy could be anywhere in the world. And not telling the authorities about it?" He rubbed his forehead. "Pen, when I told you to be careful with SPYder, this is exactly why."

"So you're SPYder?" Michael gave Pen a sly grin. "I knew it. Nobody else in school thinks like you, Pen Grey Reyes. But why do you call it SPYder?"

She warmed at his compliment. "It's not important right now." Pen turned back to her older brother. "Come on, Archie. Surely you have some ideas on how to track down the trophy?"

Archie gave a high laugh, one Pen only heard when her

brother was nervous, which wasn't often. "Of course I have ideas. But what happens if we start to look into this?" His face grew stern. "After this summer, I don't know if we should be messing around with this. I thought SPYder would keep you occupied with something safer. Mamá and Dad would kill me if anything happened to you two."

Quin laid his glasses on the table and ran his fingers through his hair, making it stick up just like Archie's. Pen bit her lip. Her twin only did this when he felt stressed. Still, she hoped Quin was on board with this. She needed his help.

"Archie," Quin said quietly. "Mariana's life is already in danger." Mariana stared at the table. Her hair fell across her cheek, hiding her eyes. "Am I right?"

Slowly, Mariana looked up. Her sea green eyes glistened. She swallowed and nodded, blinking back the tears.

"Can you tell us more?" Archie asked.

Mariana shook her head.

Archie exhaled and glared at his younger siblings. "Can you two promise me you'll stay out of trouble if I look into this a little?"

Pen nodded eagerly. Archie rolled his eyes. "Try to be a little more subtle, Penhead."

Michael snickered. "Nice nickname."

She glared at Michael. "I promise I won't look for trouble."

Archie shook his head. "That's not really what I asked."

"We promise," Quin said. "If we find any information, we can always go to the police—"

"No," Mariana said.

"I mean, we can tell you and then decide what to do," he amended.

Pen held her breath and watched her older brother. His eyes sparked. He couldn't resist a challenge. "Okay. I'll run some searches on the web and see if I can isolate any mention of the Ballon d'Or that's out of the ordinary."

"Whoa. Big Brother's watching," Michael said. "That's

like, real spy stuff."

"*Gracias.*" Pen took a deep breath and gave Archie a huge smile.

Mariana leaned over and gave Archie a quick kiss on the cheek. "Thank you, Archie. You really are a genie."

Archie's cheeks turned red. "I think you mean genius, but, yeah, you're welcome."

9

They barely made it back to St. Mary's on time for the Friendship Cup parent meeting. The four soccer players raced around the school to the side entrance of the gym. Michael tossed a "see ya" over his shoulder and jogged to his mother, who sat on the bleachers next to Lyla's parents.

"Papai," Mariana said, sounding dismayed. Her father stood away from the other parents, arms crossed and foot tapping impatiently. A thin woman hovered nearby. Mariana hurried over without saying goodbye to the twins. Quin frowned as Mariana's father straightened and spoke harshly in Portuguese. Mariana shrank an inch or two and stepped closer to her mother.

"Hey, you two." Dad's voice cut across the hubbub in the gym. Adam Grey waved at the them from a few rows up the bleachers. He motioned for them to join him.

"Where have you been? Your mother said you stayed at school after practice. I've been roaming the halls looking for you. I almost called Sister Doris."

Dad crossed his arms and looked down his nose at them. Their father was hardly ever stern, but since the summer, he'd been more vigilant.

Quin hated lying, especially to his parents. It never seemed to work out well. Before his sister could jump in with some story, he decided to tell the truth. "We went to see Archie."

Their father's eyebrows shot up. "Alone? On the metro? Without asking?"

"We took Michael and Mariana with us," Pen added. She gave Quin a frustrated look. He was sure she'd had an elaborate story ready.

"We asked him to help us do some research. We're studying the American Revolution in class and I want to narrow down my search results." Not necessarily a lie. That afternoon he'd typed American Revolution into the search bar of a classroom computer and it returned a stunning 75 million results. He made a mental note to ask Archie to help him narrow that down.

"We wanted to show Mariana more of Boston," Pen said. "And Michael tagged along." She couldn't keep a hint of irritation out of her voice. Quin looked around the gym, where the Fall Fest would be held next month. Michael waved from the bleachers. His mom, her hair a shocking bleached blond, leaned over and smoothed a wisp of curl from his forehead. Michael stopped waving and pushed his mother's hand down, a disgusted look on his face.

"Looks like Mariana didn't tell her parents what you were up to, either," Adam Grey said. He nodded toward the gym door. Mariana's father wore the same stern expression he had the day before when the twins visited Mariana's apartment. They couldn't hear the words he spoke to his daughter, but Mariana stared at her sandals and nodded. A tall, thin woman with light hair like Mariana's put a hand on Mariana's father's arm.

"Oops," Quin said. "We didn't think—"

"No," their father replied. "You didn't and after last summer—" He seemed about to launch into a lecture, but Coach Sikes called all the parents and players together. The twins exchanged relieved glances. Saved.

Coach Sikes launched into a speech about the privileges of being invited to the Friendship Cup and the rules of the tournament. Quin listened attentively. This was their first international tournament, even though it was being played in Boston. Pen pulled out her phone and started texting. A phone dinged down the bleachers and Michael pulled his own phone from his pocket, grinned, and typed back.

Pen's phone lit up. She blushed and her thumbs moved rapidly over the screen. Quin shook his head. Two months ago he and Michael only talked about soccer. Now his best friend texted his sister and asked another girl to the dance. In front of them, Mariana and her parents had taken seats on the front row of bleachers.

Quin examined a bruise on his shin and frowned. He should be excited about the tournament, but worry tugged at him. What if Archie's search returned something? And the note in his soccer ball had warned them to stay away from Mariana. Weren't they doing the opposite? And who left the note?

"We'll have strict rules about leaving the fields," Coach Sikes said. Quin realized he'd stopped listening and had probably missed a lot of important details. He shook his head and focused.

"Anyone breaking these rules will miss playing time. There will be no exceptions." He stared down each player in turn. Quin returned the coach's gaze with a firm nod.

"I thought this was supposed to be fun," Pen groaned next to him.

Coach Sikes asked for questions. Quin raised his hand. "Who are we playing?"

The coach beamed at him. "Great question, Grey Reyes. We get three games. I got the schedule this afternoon. We'll take on a team out of New York, a British team, and—" he swung his gaze to Mariana and her parents. "Our newest member's old club, the Santos out of Brazil."

A collective gasp shot through the gym. "All right," Michael shouted, punching the air. "Bring on the Brazilians."

"We're playing Mariana's old team?" Pen asked. Quin was glad to see she was finally paying attention.

"Brazil has the best goal scorers in the world." Quin thought about how hard Mariana shot the ball. He tried to imagine a whole team of Marianas and felt his stomach flip-flop.

"Doesn't it seem suspicious the Santos are playing in the Friendship Cup after Mariana showed up at school?" Pen whispered.

Quin stared down the bleachers at Mariana. She sat completely still, her hands clasped so tightly in her lap, she might have been a statue. Her mother stood up abruptly and grasped Mariana's hand, pulling the girl with her.

"*Desculpe. Temos que ir.* Sick." She motioned to her stomach. "*Obrigada,*" she said and hurried out of the gym with Mariana on her heels. Mariana's father stood up, a smile on his face, and followed his wife and daughter without a word.

"Anybody get that?" Coach Sikes asked. "Never mind. If you'll all turn in your permission slips, we'll be done."

The bleachers erupted as parents filed down to hand in the slips and teammates whooped and played tag in the gym. Only Pen and Quin kept their seats.

"Why do you think Mariana and her parents took off?" Quin asked, his eyes on the doorway.

His twin shook her head, making her long ponytail almost smack him in the face. "Mariana didn't like it when Coach announced we'd play the Santos."

Quin nodded. "But her father didn't mind. He seemed..." He searched for the word. Not happy, but something else. "Smug. But why did they leave before they signed the permission slip? Mariana can't play in the tournament until it's signed." He didn't add his next thought. He didn't think they could beat the Santos without Mariana. He wasn't sure they could win with her, either.

"First that strange man at practice, then the way her father acted when he answered the door yesterday. Now this," Pen mused.

"Don't forget my soccer ball and the note." The worry

that had been gnawing at his stomach now felt like a gaping hole.

"I think there's something Mariana isn't telling us, even though she wants us to help." His sister's face lit up. "Ohhh, or something she *can't* tell us."

Quin stared at her, feeling the gnawing in his stomach growing larger. "Like what?"

She shrugged and looked around the gym to make sure no one was nearby. Their father was talking to Michael's mother. When he saw the twins, he half waved and mouthed, "I'm coming," before turning back to his conversation.

Pen lowered her voice and leaned into Quin. "We have to go to Mariana's and see if we can find any clues."

"You mean spy on her?" He felt his legs go shaky. The last thing he wanted to do was sneak into Mariana's house, especially if her father was around. "I thought we were trying to help her."

"We are. How can we help her if she isn't telling us everything? Besides, I've been reading about spies for my project—"

"You're already working on that?" Quin couldn't help but feel impressed. Usually Pen waited until the last minute.

She frowned. "Yes, but listen. Sometimes those spies had to play both sides to gain all the information they needed. It'll be sort of like we're double agents. We'll look for the trophy, but we'll try to figure out what's going on with Mariana too."

Pen hopped lightly down the bleachers and jogged to Adam Grey, waving at Michael. Quin watched, feeling like a spider had just woven a cobweb into his already upset stomach. He stumbled down the bleachers on shaky legs.

"Ready for the tournament next week?" Coach Sikes asked as Quin reached the gym floor.

"Sure."

"Are you feeling okay, Grey Reyes? You look a little pale.

Did you and da Silva eat the same lunch?"

"Yeah, that's probably it. Bad tacos."

He wished it was food causing his stomach to twist in knots. Whatever plan his twin had in mind, he was sure it would land them in the middle of a web of trouble.

The next morning the Saints had a game against the Middle High Lions, a team they quickly dispatched with a flurry of goals in the first half. Coach Sikes pulled Quin out of the goal the second half to let Dennis play. Pen and Mariana also joined him on the bench. Michael stayed in the game as one of the few older players. Across the field, Dad cheered as the Saints mounted another attack. Pen pointed out Mariana's father to Quin. He stood away from the other parents, at the far end of the field. He seemed as irritated as he had when he answered Pen's knock on the door.

"Your mom couldn't make it?" Pen asked Mariana, who sat at the end of the bench, leaving a space between her and Pen. Mariana frowned and shrugged. "She had to work."

"My mom works some Saturdays, too."

"Cleaning offices?" Mariana shot back.

"No," Pen stammered. "She's usually working on a lecture or studying some artifact."

Mariana said nothing to this. Quin shook his head. One thing Pen definitely was not was smooth. He watched Michael split two defenders with a pass Luca would be proud of. The fifth grader who ran to the ball shot it wide of the goal.

"Nice going," he muttered on the other side of Pen. "Is this part of your plan to get us invited over?"

She shook her head. "No, I thought—" she broke off and stiffened. "Look. Isn't that the same man who tried to grab Mariana the other day? The man in black?"

Quin stopped knocking dirt from his cleats and scanned the other sideline. A man dressed all in black approached

Mariana's father, who glanced at the man and turned back to the game. Quin couldn't tell if they were speaking from this distance. He adjusted his glasses, but he still couldn't be sure this was the same man who'd grabbed Mariana.

"Maybe." He leaned over to see past his sister. Mariana kicked a rock under the bench, staring at the ground. She didn't seem to notice her father had a visitor. Or maybe, Quin thought, she's trying to act unconcerned. Mariana's eyes flicked up, her glance so quick he would have missed it if he hadn't been paying attention. He leaned back, certain Mariana also knew the man was at the game.

He gave Pen a brief nod of assent. She fidgeted next to him, drumming her fingers on the bench, her cleats dancing up and down.

"Grey Reyes," Coach Sikes said, making both twins jump. "Why don't you go work off some of that excess energy and give Blalock a breather?"

Pen hopped up and jogged to the centerline to sub for Michael. Quin risked a glance at Mariana and found the girl's breathtaking eyes boring into him.

"What?"

"You have a spider on your shoulder."

Quin shrieked and leaped up, hopping in a circle as he batted his shoulder. The crowd shouted from the other side and Quin stopped dancing in time to see little Dennis Leary make a diving save Salvatore Cienfuegos himself would be proud of. Then he realized half his teammates were staring at him.

"Are you trying to help the other team score?" Coach Sikes asked.

Quin felt his face redden. "No, sorry. There was a spider—"

"Sit down," his coach ordered. "If I need a distraction, I'll let you know."

The other Saints on the bench snickered. Quin plopped onto the hard wood, mortified.

"At least," Mariana said from the end of the bench, "you

saved the spider." She pointed to a tiny brown spider scur-rying away from the dirt into the grassy refuge of the field.

"I hate spiders."

Mariana's mouth curved into a smile. "Me too."

Quin smiled back. Then he glanced at the far side of the field. The man in black and Mariana's father were gone.

10

After the game, Dad insisted they eat lunch at a nearby deli, even though Pen told him they had plans to hang out with Mariana.

"Invite her along," Adam Grey said.

Mariana had thrown her gear bag over her shoulder and was halfway across the field to the road. Pen had to race to catch her. She explained the lunch invitation quickly.

"*Eu não sei*," Mariana said, chewing on her bottom lip. By now Pen was used to the Portuguese phrase for 'I don't know.' "My father wanted me to go home after the game."

"We'll go with you," Pen said brightly. "And he'd want you to eat lunch, right? Plus," she added, leaning in, "you'll be with us when Archie tells us the results of his search."

Quin and Dad walked up, cutting off Mariana's reply.

"Mariana, have you ever had a corned beef sandwich on rye?" Dad asked.

Mariana shook her head. Dad put a palm on his forehead in mock dismay. "Then it's settled. You're coming with us." He motioned for the group to follow him. "A good sandwich can help you conquer the world."

Pen rolled her eyes, but Mariana smiled. "*Bom*," she said. "One sandwich."

Pen checked her phone incessantly through lunch until Dad threatened to take it away. "I noticed Quin hasn't looked at his once," he added with a nod of approval. Pen frowned at him but tucked her phone into her bag without a word. Quin hadn't told their parents his phone was missing. He at least had the decency to look a little embarrassed at their father's praise.

Archie hadn't texted her yet about his web search for the Ballon d'Or and she couldn't stop thinking about the man they'd seen at the soccer game. Why was he following Mariana and her father? Why had Mariana's father gone with him? What did he want?

Finally, after sandwiches, chips, and chocolate chip cookies for dessert, Dad said he needed to stop by his office for awhile.

"Can we go to Mariana's?" Pen blurted out.

"Pen, it's rude to invite yourself over." Dad turned to Mariana. "I thought your mother was working today?"

"*Sim*, but she will be home soon. And my father is..." she trailed off, but Dad seemed not to notice. Pen could tell his mind was already on his own work.

"Besides, we'll be right here in the neighborhood," Pen added, glad Mariana's apartment building was so close to the school.

Dad sighed. "How much trouble can you three get into in one afternoon?"

It was a joke, but both Pen and Quin heard the edge of caution in it, something that hadn't existed before their escapade in Mexico and Spain.

"Don't answer that," Dad said. "Just promise me you'll mind—"

"Your P's and Q's," the twins finished. "We will," Quin added. Pen didn't echo this sentiment.

Once Dad left, Pen checked her phone again. Still no sign of life from Archie, though SPYder had two new messages in its inbox. Pen held off on reading them. She already had a mission. She needed to get inside Mariana's house and see if she could find anything that might point to a possible suspect for who stole the trophy, without Mariana realizing it, of course.

They headed down the street with soccer bags slung over their shoulders. Mariana took the lead and they cut through the park and past St. Mary's. A couple of times, the hair on the back of Pen's neck prickled and she swung around to look behind them.

"What?" her brother whispered as they waited to cross the same street where he had nearly been run over. They'd chosen to use the crosswalk this time.

She shook her head slowly. "Nothing. I think." She stared down the street. Nobody on the sidewalk looked unusual or familiar.

They walked inside the building and up to the third floor. Pen got ahead of Quin and Mariana, who'd both stopped so Quin could admire the brickwork of an original wall. She could hear her brother describing the unique architecture of the building, something he'd picked up from Mamá in their travels. Well, perhaps he'd be an architect someday, but right now Mariana was probably listening politely and realizing what a nerd Quin was. Pen paused outside the apartment door. She heard the dull thud of footfalls on the other side. She hoped it was Mariana's mother. She didn't want to face Mariana's father right now.

Mariana and Quin arrived and the Brazilian girl grabbed the doorknob, ready to insert her key, but the knob turned beneath her fingers.

"*Estranho*. Mamãe always tells me to lock the door, but she didn't."

"I think your mother's home," Pen said. "Or your dad. I heard footsteps on the other side."

Mariana chewed her lip, her hand frozen on the knob. "My mother said she would be late. And my father... I do not think..." She hesitated and glanced around. Pen remembered the prickling feeling she'd had, like they were being watched. Goosebumps popped up on her arms. She felt inside her bag and produced a soccer cleat.

"What's that for? Are you going to knock someone out with the smell?" Quin pulled one of the school's old soccer balls he'd borrowed out of his bag. Mariana gave them both a strange look and opened the door.

A single window in the living room funneled the bright afternoon sunshine into a blinding beam of light. Still, Pen glimpsed a shadow and a flutter of movement at the window. She shaded her eyes with the soccer cleat and bounded across the room in time to hear a loud clang. A breeze blew into her face from the open window.

Pen stuck her head out the window. A fire escape zigzagged down the side of the building, ending about six feet from the ground. Traffic rumbled three stories below, people waited at the bus stop and meandered down the street. Most of Mission Hill seemed to be enjoying the warm September afternoon. Pen felt it again, the whisper in the back of her mind. She looked up.

Two stories above her head, a dark shadow climbed toward the roof.

"Someone's up there." She clambered through the window and started climbing the escape ladder. The metal rattled beneath her hands and her feet echoed on the rungs. The person above Pen paused and looked down. She glimpsed a suit, a craggy face, dark eyes. Then the man rushed up the ladder. His legs disappeared over the edge of the roof.

"Pen, wait," Quin called out beneath her. She glanced down at her brother and caught a dizzying glimpse of the sidewalk below. She swallowed hard and continued to scramble up the ladder, past the fourth and fifth floor apartments. The metal rungs vibrated inside her clenched fists. Someone was climbing up after her.

Pen reached the roof and peered over the edge. The sun glared off the cement, nearly blinding her. She hauled herself over the low wall and tumbled onto the flat rooftop. The hot cement burned her bare knees and Pen yelped and leaped to her feet. She still had her soccer cleat in her hand, but she was alone on the roof except for two pigeons, who watched her from the far end, heads cocked and feathers ruffled. One cooed at Pen as if asking what she was doing up there.

Then the ladder clanged against the side of the bricks and Quin scrambled onto the roof with her.

"Ow, hot." He stood quickly and blew on his hands.

"There was someone here," Pen said before Quin could tear into her about what a stupid idea this had been. "I saw him climb over the top."

"*Está tudo bem*?" Mariana called from below. Pen leaned over the rooftop to wave at the girl. A bus squealed on the street below and she couldn't help but imagine falling from this height onto the top of it. Her stomach churned and she leaned back, suddenly faint. She sank to the hot cement and took a few deep breaths.

"Where did he go?" Some apartment buildings in Boston had rooftop gardens and terraces. Not this one. It held nothing but broken bricks and pigeon poop. Then she spied the half-sized door built into the roof.

"There." Pen stood up and jogged around a pile of discarded bricks and tugged the door handle. It opened to an empty stairwell leading back down into the apartment building.

"He might still be on the stairs," Quin said as joined her.

"Or at Mariana's." They rushed down two flights of stairs and found themselves in Mariana's hallway. The door to the apartment was locked.

"Mariana!" Pen pounded on the door. "Are you okay? Let us in."

The deadbolt clicked loudly and the door swung open. "What happened?" Mariana cried as the twins hurried inside. "I didn't want to climb up so high."

"We didn't see anyone," Quin said.

"But there was someone there," Pen insisted. "I saw him. Or at least, his shoe." She dropped the soccer cleat back into her bag.

"We should call the police," Quin said. "What if he stole something?" The twins looked around for the first time. Besides a narrow couch, nothing decorated the tiny living room except a few boxes.

"No police," Mariana said, looking around the apartment. "What will we tell them? Someone wanted to steal empty boxes and clothes?"

"But someone was here," Quin said. "He must have wanted something..."

"*Seu irmão*," Mariana grimaced and spoke in English. "Your brother, did he find anything?"

Pen pulled her phone from her pocket only to find a blank screen. No texts or alerts from Archie. Strange. She texted him for an update. "Nothing yet, but don't worry, he'll find something soon. Maybe you should give me your phone number. That way I can call you if I hear anything."

"I share a phone with my mother," Mariana said flatly.

"Oh."

"Nothing wrong with not having a phone," Quin defended Mariana. Pen snorted.

"You only say that because you've never liked having one."

"Mamãe is scared of phones. She thinks a phone makes it easy to find us."

"Is someone looking for you? Is that why that man was here?" Quin asked.

Mariana shrugged but didn't reply.

Pen's phone buzzed. She checked the text. Michael, not Archie.

Let's get some practice 2moro. Park at 2?

Normally Pen would feel more excited to spend time with Michael, but right now she couldn't be distracted. She shoved her phone back into her pocket and gave Mariana her best Maria Grey Reyes impression, the look Mamá often used on Pen when she knew her daughter was leaving details out of a story.

"Mariana, why did you ask us to help you find the Ballon d'Or for Luca if you're not going to tell us the truth?"

"Pen." Quin shook his head and frowned at her. She frowned back.

Mariana looked back and forth. "Are you two fighting?"

"No," they said at the same time, so forcefully Mariana took a step back. Quin sighed and said. "If you want us to help you find the trophy, you should tell us everything you know about it."

"I did," Mariana said, not convincingly.

Pen got an idea. "Do you have anything Luca gave you? Maybe it will help you remember something about the trophy?"

"Come to my room." The Brazilian girl disappeared into one of the two rooms off the living room. Inside, the twins found her sitting on a narrow bed. Two suitcases lay open on the floor, half unpacked. Pen spotted a pair of leather sandals and more of those tank tops Mariana sported outside of her St. Mary's school uniform.

She tugged a photo album out of one of the suitcases, one filled with actual photos. Pen gaped. She kept all her digital photos organized in file folders on her computer, in her secret folder of course. Just in case Dad or Archie got any ideas about posting any embarrassing photos on social sites.

Mariana sat down and flipped through a few pictures, then held out the album. Quin pushed a lock of brown hair away from his glasses and studied the picture. Pen leaned over to see the photo.

"Is this you?" Quin pointed to a young girl in a bright red sundress, her hair a sun-kissed blond. An older boy draped one arm across her shoulder and grinned at the camera. He wore only a pair of blue swim trunks and rested one bare foot on top of a worn soccer ball. Behind them a white beach sparkled and waves toppled toward the sand.

"*Sim*. Me and Luca as kids. Luca lived with us after my grandparents died."

Quin's mouth dropped open. "Wow, oh wow. Wait 'til I tell Michael about this." He started flipping through other photos and Mariana paused to tell him where each was taken. Pen half listened and cased the room, but it was as bare as the living room. No clues to find here. Nothing for the intruder to steal. Unless... maybe he wasn't trying to steal something. Maybe he wanted to steal... someone? Pen cast a hard look at Mariana, remembering how nervous she'd been when they walked in.

Quin flipped to the next picture and gasped. "I can't believe it," he whispered. He pulled a photo from the album and waved it at Mariana. "Is this Luca with Salvatore Cienfuegos?"

He flattened the picture on the bed and Pen walked over, drawn in by his enthusiasm. This was a recent photo. Luca wore a white tuxedo instead of his Real Madrid jersey. And next to Luca, towering over the footballer like a laughing giant, was Quin's idol. A red bowtie matched the goalkeeper's unmistakable red hair and he had his arm around Luca's shoulder. Both soccer players laughed at the camera like they'd just shared an inside joke.

"Oh, *sim*. That is at a charity event last year. They're friends."

Pen could see her brother's head spinning at the news. "This means, it means."

"Yeah, yeah, it means you're just three degrees away from Salvatore Cienfuegos, we get it," Pen said.

"Do you have more pictures?" Quin asked.

Mariana shrugged. "Perhaps." She went back to her suitcase and pulled out a camera with a zoom lens. His eyebrows shot up. "Nice. Do you like photography?"

Mariana flashed a rare smile. "Yes. Do you?"

Pen groaned. "You're not going to have an in-depth conversation about taking pictures, are you?"

"Oh, like you and Archie and Dad never have the most boring talks about computers." Quin turned back to Mariana. "So what's your favorite type of photography?"

Pen sighed, frustrated. Mariana hadn't actually told them anything. Why was she just showing them pictures of Luca? At least she could have a look around the apartment while Quin kept Mariana and himself distracted.

"Could I use your bathroom? Too much lemonade at lunch." Pen tried to look uncomfortable. Now that she thought about it, she did have to go.

"*Claro*. It's between my room and my parents'."

"Thanks." Pen ducked back into the living room. She walked past the bathroom and glanced into the other bedroom. Besides a bed and suitcases, it held nothing interesting either. Pen stared at the empty closets. It didn't look like Mariana's family planned on being here long. Either that or they didn't like to unpack.

She heard the front door bolt sliding open and dashed into the living room just as the door opened and Mariana's father stepped inside. When he saw Pen, he drew up short.

"What are you doing here?" He shut the door and moved toward Pen. She took an uncertain step toward Mariana's room.

"You're the other forward," her father said. "I watched you play this morning. You're good."

"Oh," Pen said, confused. "Thanks."

Mariana's father shrugged. "Not as good as my Mariana."

Heat flew into Pen's face. It was bad enough to lose her starting position to Mariana. She didn't need anyone telling her Mariana was a better soccer player.

"Papai," Mariana said from the doorway to her room. She turned to Pen, her cheeks as red as Pen's felt. "*Desculpá-lo*. He thinks nobody is as good as me or Luca."

Her father shrugged. "I am right, at least, about Luca."

"Papai, when we came home, someone was here." Mariana gestured to the window and fire escape. "He left that way. Pen and Quin followed him.”

Mariana’s father frowned and crossed the room to look out the window. When he turned back to them, his face was unreadable. “I do not think so.”

“But we saw him,” Pen protested. “I followed him to the roof, but we lost him.”

Mariana’s father glared at her. “Probably just a teenager. You should not be on the fire escape.”

“But maybe you should call the police,” Quin said.

“I think it is time for your friends to leave.” Mariana’s father opened the apartment door.

Mariana shot them a helpless look.

Quin grabbed his soccer bag and shoved Pen’s at her.

“Where did you go?” Pen asked Mariana’s father. “I saw you watching the game this morning. You left.” She didn’t mention the man in black.

“Pen. Let’s go.” Her brother pushed her toward the open door until they were standing in the hall.

Mariana’s father glared at Pen, but his expression shifted to smugness. “It is not your business, as you say, but I go to *futebol* practice.”

Pen shook her head. “Soccer practice? But our game was this morning. Do you mean you’re playing on a team?”

Mariana’s father laughed. “I will help coach the Santos in the tournament. They arrived yesterday. We had our first practice this morning.”

Quin’s mouth dropped open. “You’re coaching the Santos in the tournament? The same team Luca played for before he went to Real Madrid? But they’re amazing.”

This time Mariana’s father smiled. “*Claro.* And after watching your game, I do not think we will have any trouble winning the tournament.” He slammed the door.

“What a jerk,” Quin said. “But he’s probably right about the tournament.”

Pen’s phone buzzed. She tugged it from her pocket. Archie’s signature α blinked at her.

α: Meet me at home pronto. Don’t tell Mariana. No time to

explain.

Pen blinked at the strange text.

"Is it Archie?" Quin asked. They headed downstairs.

She nodded. "He wants to meet us ASAP. And to keep it a secret from Mariana."

"That won't be a problem." Quin glanced up at the empty fire escape. "And we're not the only ones keeping a secret."

Pen stopped walking. "What do you mean?"

"I saw someone in one of those photos in Mariana's albums."

"Who?"

Quin turned to look at Pen, his eyes as serious as she'd ever seen.

"The man in black. He's in the background in the photo of Luca and Salvatore Cienfuegos."

11

Archie wasn't at the house when Pen and Quin got home. Dad was still at the office and the door to Mamá's study was shut. Pen mumbled something about researching spies and went to her room. Quin didn't follow. He felt uneasy about the way Mariana's father reacted to their story about the man on the roof. He wandered through the house, stopped in the kitchen to grab a banana, then found himself in his art studio. Late afternoon sunlight filtered through the windows, creating the quality of light Quin loved.

He examined a half-finished painting of Salvatore Cienfuegos he'd been working on over the summer. The famous keeper arced through the air in his signature red jersey and black shorts, his arms outstretched. Quin hadn't painted the goalkeeper's face yet because faces were difficult things to capture. He thought about the photo of Luca and Cienfuegos in Mariana's album and the smiles of his two favorite soccer players. He still couldn't believe Mariana was lucky enough to know them both.

The image of the man in black popped into his head. In Mariana's album, he'd seen two pictures of the man—once in the background of the photo with Luca and Cienfuegos dressed in tuxedos. In the other photo, the man wore a light khaki button down shirt and thick black hair covered his head instead of the black cap he'd worn at the soccer field, but Quin felt sure this was the same man. He'd stood next to Mariana's father with a soccer stadium in the background and frowned at the camera just like he'd frowned at them the first day of soccer practice. Who was he? How did Mariana know him? Why was he at the game the other day?

Quin thought about the missing trophy, the world famous, gold plated soccer ball. The man in black must be involved, but did that mean Mariana was involved somehow, too? How much did they actually know about the Brazilian girl?

He sat down at his desk and grabbed a sketchpad and a charcoal pencil. While he mulled over the stolen trophy, he drew clear black lines on the paper. Soon, he was fully absorbed in the sketch, forgetting about the man in black, the stolen trophy and SPYder. A phone rang somewhere in the house. Quin ignored it.

A rap on the door snapped him out of his zone. Archie leaned against the doorframe, the house phone Mamá and Dad insisted on keeping in his hand. "What are you working on, Michelangelo?"

Quin shook his head, coming out of his daze. "Just doing a little sketching."

Archie walked to the desk to have a look. "A little?" He raised one black eyebrow, a gesture Pen often mimicked. Quin had never been able to get his eyebrows to move independently of each other. One more thing he couldn't do that his siblings could.

Quin looked down at the drawing. A soccer ball balanced on top of a rocky pedestal. As far as sketches go, it was simple. Still, he'd shaded the ball to suggest the gleam of light off gold and carefully penciled in the words BALLON D'OR into the base. He shrugged. "It'd look better in color. Or as a model," he added as an afterthought.

Archie nodded and slapped him on the back. "It looks amazing to me. Better than the stick figures I can draw."

He handed the phone to Quin. "I almost forgot. I put her on hold. And we're meeting in your room right after you finish this call."

"Her? Who? And why my room?"

Archie gave Quin his signature lopsided grin. "Yeah. Her. As in a girl on the phone for you. And for some reason, Mamá thinks we're up to something if we meet in mine or Pen's rooms, so yours it is."

Quin didn't bother to say Mamá was usually right. He stared at the phone in his hand. Who would call him on the house phone? And a girl? It must be Mariana. Perhaps she'd thought of something else to tell them about the trophy. Or she'd realized Quin had flipped through her photos and seen the man in black and wanted to confront him. Quin felt sweat break out on his forehead. Why was Mariana calling the house phone instead of Pen's cell?

"Don't talk long, killer. We need you for the meeting." Archie laughed and left the studio.

Quin lifted the phone to his ear, his heart in his throat.

"H-hello? Mariana?"

"No." Anna Callahan's voice came through the receiver. "This isn't Mariana."

Quin felt his heart stop. "Ahhh—" he said.

"Sorry? I didn't catch that."

He cleared his throat. "Hey, Anna. Are you looking for Pen?"

"If I wanted to talk to Pen, I'd call her phone," Anna said, her voice still cool. "She gave me this number in case she got grounded and I needed to talk to her."

"Oh, right." This sounded plausible, except Pen wasn't grounded, and Anna was calling him. He tapped his forehead with the charcoal pencil still in his hand. "So, what's up?"

"I was thinking about our project on the Revolution for Mr. Hardy. Remember we have to present the outline of our ideas on Monday."

"Sure," Quin said, racking his brain. He'd had trouble

paying attention the last few days thinking about Luca da Silva and the golden ball. He was pretty sure he and Michael had held a whispered argument about whether Salvatore Cienfuegos should have won the trophy instead, but they hadn't talked about the project.

"Well, I know you'll do something with art and I can do some poetry. And Michael can... find something, I'm sure."

"Yeah, sounds good," Quin said.

"Great," Anna responded, her voice bright. "Let's get together tomorrow afternoon and talk about it. Want to meet me at D'lite Donuts around three?"

Quin opened and closed his mouth several times. He couldn't get his voice to work.

"Yeah."

Yeah? Couldn't he come up with anything else to say?

"Perfect, see you then. Oh, and would you mind not mentioning this to Pen? She might want to come and since it's for class we should probably focus on the assignment and you know how she can be..." Anna suddenly grew quiet.

"No, I get it," Quin said. "I won't tell."

"Great. See you tomorrow. Bye!" Anna rushed through the words. The phone clicked off and started beeping in Quin's ear. He dropped it on his desk in a daze. What had just happened? In the back of Quin's mind, he knew he was supposed to be somewhere doing something. What was it? He stared at his drawing, thinking about Anna sitting in front of him in class. Could he ask her to the Fall Fest Dance tomorrow? Just the thought of it made his stomach feel like a cold lump of clay.

"Quintus Grey Reyes," Pen shouted through the house. "Get up here."

That's right. He was supposed to be in his room with Pen and Archie. His other secret meeting. The thought made his legs feel weak. He had a secret meeting with a girl tomorrow. Anna Callahan. Suddenly Quin came to life. He mimed kicking a soccer ball and punched the air.

"Goal," he said to the faceless Salvatore Cienfuegos. "Not even you could save that."

"What'd you do, go out for tacos?" Archie quipped when Quin walked into his own room. Archie was stretched out on the bed with his tennis shoes still on. He pointed to his watch.

"Finally. Took you long enough." Pen sat cross legged in the window seat with her laptop open.

Quin shut the door to his room and the door to the adjoining bathroom.

"What's wrong with you? Your face is red."

"Nothing." He responded too quickly, but in his head he could still hear Anna's melodic voice. "Don't tell Pen. You know how she can be." Quin cleared his throat.

"I was drawing in the sunroom. It was a little warm in there." He hoped for once Archie would keep his mouth shut.

"Sure it wasn't the girl on the phone warming you up?" His older brother put his arms behind his head and reclined against the pillow, giving Quin a lazy smile.

Quin sighed. Was it too much to ask for some brotherly honor?

"What girl?"

Pen sat up straight, the laptop forgotten.

"Someone from school, to talk about a school assignment."

Pen narrowed her eyes. She knew every kid in their grade, just like Quin. He wondered if she was mentally ticking off the girls in his class. How long would it take to get to Anna?

"Don't we have other things to talk about? Like that note in my soccer ball? Or Archie's search for the Ballon d'Or? I mean, your text was kind of weird." Quin turned to Archie when he said this. "Meet me ASAP. Don't tell Mariana?"

Archie sat up. "You're right, Q. Why waste time talking

about girls when there's a mystery afoot? No offense, Pen-head."

"Just tell us what you found," Pen pleaded.

Archie shook his head. "You first. What note is Quin talking about?"

She pulled the note from her pocket and read the brief message again.

"Stay away from Mariana and her family, or you'll lose more than your soccer ball."

The words still sent a shiver through Quin. He listened to his sister's quick explanation of Quin's busted soccer ball, leaving out the part where he almost got run over. Then she told Archie about the man on the fire escape and Mariana's dad's reaction. She left out the chase to the roof. Quin frowned at her from his desk, but he didn't jump in.

Archie sat up on the bed. "That's some story." The skin crinkled between his brow like it did when he was trying to solve a difficult equation. "You said Mariana and her father were both home when you found the soccer ball? That means they didn't leave the note. Someone else is involved."

"I should have thought of that.

"But why wouldn't someone want us to spend time with Mariana? Nobody else knows we're helping her look for the trophy," Quin said.

Archie shrugged.

"What did you find out in your web search? I can't stand it any longer," Pen said.

Archie sat back down on Quin's bed, crossing his long legs like a pretzel. The twins joined him so all three sat in a triangle, something they used to do when they were little and held midnight powwows after their parents went to bed.

"So after you four left MIT, I did some searching. I knew I'd have to look for more than just 'Ballon d'Or' and 'Luca.' There's millions of articles on the internet related to those two, and I found out some interesting things about

Mariana's family." He paused and waited for his siblings to beg for more information.

"What?" they both cried, giving him exasperated looks.

"For starters, Mariana's father was arrested in Brazil."

Pen gasped. "For what?"

"Fixing soccer matches. The article I found said he was an assistant coach with the Santos and he paid players to lose games."

"Lose games?" Pen shook her head. "Why would anyone want to lose?

Quin couldn't imagine accepting any amount of money to lose a game, but he nodded. "I've read about this. Players lose on purpose to 'throw' the game. They let the other team win so the people who bet on them win money. Match-fixing is a huge problem in international soccer."

"The article I read said Luca transferred to Madrid after his uncle was arrested. He didn't want to play for the Santos after that. Can't say I blame him."

"But her dad is here," Quin said. "Coaching Mariana's old team."

Archie nodded. "It said they never had enough evidence to put him in jail so the police released him, but it also said they had more suspects in the match-fixing, but no arrests were ever made."

"Poor Mariana. No wonder she moved to Boston."

Pen's brothers looked at her like she'd said she wanted to become a ballerina.

"What?" Pen shrugged. "Her father was arrested, her uncle left for Spain, and now she's stuck at St. Mary's with Sister Doris. I feel sorry for her."

Archie and Quin exchanged a look, both amazed at Pen's rare display of empathy.

"But, what does all this have to do with the trophy being stolen?" Pen asked.

"Right," Archie said. "My first search returned millions of articles, and nothing useful. That's why it took me so long."

Only Archie would think taking a few days to search for something on the web was a long time. "So what did you do?" Quin asked.

Archie winked. "I decided to dig deep."

Pen smiled. "A deep web search. Of course."

Quin shook his head. "A what?"

Archie took on Mamá's professorial look and Quin geared himself up for one of his big brother's I-know-more-than-you-ever-will lectures.

"The deep web contains all kinds of information not normally returned on a regular web search. When you type a search word into a normal browser, you're only skimming the surface of information on that topic, usually the most popular and most common." Archie spread his arms out to illustrate, looking like a Buddha in his cross-legged position. An annoying one.

"A deep web search is the difference between the surface of the ocean and what lies deep beneath the waves. The information you find there can be..." Archie paused and cleared his throat. "Enlightening."

Quin wondered if he'd read his mind about the Buddha thing.

"It can also be a holding ground for all kinds of nefarious activities," Pen said brightly. Archie shot her a questioning look. "Which is why I never use it," she added.

"Hmm. I hope not, *hermanita*. That stuff can be dangerous." His eyes held Pen's until she blinked and looked away.

Quin groaned. "Can you both get to the point?"

Archie shifted his gaze to Quin. "I found a message on a private board. It took some doing to get there. It didn't reference Luca or the Ballon d'Or, but it did talk about the golden ball and its owner."

"What did it say?" Pen asked.

Archie frowned. "Let me show you. I took a screen shot." He pulled out his phone and handed it to Pen. Quin jumped up to look over her shoulder while Pen magnified the image.

Help Wanted moving golden ball from current owner to new one. Must be willing to travel. Compensation upon sale.

Quin blinked and read the cryptic message again. "The golden ball. It sounds like the Ballon d'Or." He thought of his sketch downstairs.

Pen handed the phone back to Archie. "Travel? Does that mean they took the trophy out of Spain?"

"I thought about that, too. And this bit about compensation. It must mean they're going to sell it on the black market."

"So now we just have to figure out where the trophy is. Then we can find the thief and we'll know who's threatening Mariana's family," Pen exclaimed.

"Oh, just that?" Quin snorted. Pen seemed to think solving an international mystery was as easy as giving advice on SPYder. His sister shot him an irritated look.

"I was able to track the message's address through several networks." Pen started to interrupt but Archie waved her question away. "I won't tell you how. What's important is this: That message on the dark web didn't originate in Europe or Brazil or anywhere close to Luca and the Ballon d'Or." Archie glanced at the closed door and rubbed his brow.

Pinpricks of fear rippled down Quin's spine, raising goose bumps on his arms. "Where did it come from?"

Archie lowered his voice. "From here. That message originated in Boston."

12

The three Grey Reyes siblings stared across the triangle of legs and elbows in silence. Quin was the first to break it.

"The message was sent from Boston? What does that mean?"

Archie stood up from Quin's bed. "It means we're done with this investigation. We need to tell the police."

"No," Pen yelped. "We can't. Mariana asked us not to. If Luca goes to the police, Mariana or her family could be in danger." She didn't add this investigation was finally getting interesting.

"We're not Luca da Silva." Archie spoke sharply. "And this information was buried deep, not meant to be found."

"But how could the thief, or whoever sent this message, be in Boston?" Quin's brows wrinkled so much his hair nearly covered them.

"Mariana's only been in Boston a few weeks," Archie pointed out.

"You think Mariana sent that message?" Pen tried to picture the tall Brazilian girl writing a threatening note to her own uncle and couldn't.

"No, but obviously, there must be a connection."

The twins arrived at the same conclusion at the same time. "The man in black."

"Who?" Archie stood up and examined the twins in a

way that reminded Pen of their father.

Pen quickly described the man they'd seen after the soccer game tugging on Mariana's arm and her reaction, imploring the twins not to call the police. Quin added he'd seen the same man after their game that weekend and in Mariana's photo album. Her cheeks warm, Pen told Archie about the man they'd chased on the roof. His frown deepened.

"This isn't good. He could be the one who took the trophy."

"If he is, then Mariana knows him. She was protecting him when she asked us not to call the police," Pen said.

They all fell silent, trying to absorb this thought. She shook her head. "Why would Mariana protect the man who stole her uncle's trophy? It doesn't make sense."

Archie sighed loudly. "And you two call yourselves agents of intrigue? You're missing the obvious here."

Pinpricks of annoyance shot through Pen. Archie didn't have to act like he knew everything all the time. He nodded, prodding her toward the answer.

"Trying to protect him," she mumbled to herself. "But Mariana told us about the stolen trophy..." The answer flashed like a meteor through her mind, brief but brilliant. "Oh, she doesn't know. She doesn't know the man in black took the trophy."

"Good." Archie grinned. "Conceivably, yes."

"But," Quin said, "that means Mariana didn't want us to call the police for another reason."

Archie's grin disappeared. "I hadn't thought of that. This is exactly why we should tell the police."

"Archie, please, not yet." Pen hated begging but she'd do it not to lose the case. "Give us one more day. I can turn up some information on this, I know I can."

"How?" Her big brother sounded skeptical.

Pen racked her brain. There had to be something she could do to help find the trophy. "I'll meet Mariana tomorrow afternoon and ask her about the note we found in the soccer ball. If I can find out who sent it, maybe that will tell us who Mariana's protecting and why."

"Hmm." Archie got off the bed and paced. The wooden floorboards squeaked.

"No one knows we're looking into the Ballon d'Or, unless someone can track your web search."

"Not a chance." Archie stopped pacing. "Okay. It would be good to have a little more information before we go to the police. Maybe I can narrow down the location where the message was sent from Boston."

"Good idea." Pen felt relieved Archie was allowing more time to track down the trophy. She might have agreed to go to Eileen Esposito's birthday party at that point.

They both looked at Quin. He shrugged. "Sounds okay. I can't go with you tomorrow, though." Quin's neck and cheeks flushed red. He cleared his throat and stared out the window at the massive oak tree with a hint of fall color in its leaves.

"Quin." Pen examined her twin's face. "Why are you blushing?"

"Someone's coming." The floorboards creaked with heavy footfalls down the hall.

"Hello?" their father called out. "Are the three of you hiding in here like sardines?"

He opened the door and stuck his head in. Archie sprawled on the bed in feigned casualness. Quin flipped through his latest art magazine at his desk and Pen scanned her laptop from the window seat.

"Hmm," their father mused. "My three children, the perfect picture of innocence."

Pen looked up and blushed. Quin kept his eyes on his magazine, but Archie stood up and stretched. "Just catching up on school gossip. You know how St. Mary's is."

Dad nodded slowly. "I do. In fact, I got an email from Sister Doris today."

Pen froze. "What about?" She tried to sound casual.

"About a certain text someone sent to all the students.

An advertisement for something about a spider? I don't suppose any of you would know anything about that?"

Archie shrugged and ran a hand through his black hair. "I'm in college and way past middle school shenanigans." He gave Pen a brilliant smile. She read the challenge behind it. *See if you can get out of this one.*

Pen cleared her throat, but before she could speak, Quin piped up. "I didn't send the text, but everyone's talking about it at school. Did all the parents get the email?"

Dad nodded. "I believe so. And I know you didn't send it." His eyes shifted to Pen. Dad was phishing for information like a hacker. Well, she wouldn't be the one to give it to him.

"Ms. Morgan brought it up in class and made sure we knew texting strangers was dangerous," she said. "And I haven't texted any strangers."

Dad held her gaze for a moment and she resisted dropping her eyes or looking at Quin or Archie.

Dad sighed. "After this summer, after almost losing you two—" his gaze went from one twin to the other and his normally steady blue eyes watered. "I think your mother and I are a little too hands-off sometimes. We want to encourage your independence but—"

"Dad." Pen could tell her father was warming into a long lecture. "We're okay."

"Nothing to worry about but a little soccer drama, right?" Archie added.

Dad laughed. "The tournament. Right. Let's talk about the game plan over dinner. Your mother is picking up Italian. Let's set the table and clean up the kitchen a little before she gets home."

"Sure," Pen said, quickly followed by Archie and Quin agreeing to help.

Their father frowned and shook his head. "Everybody jumping at once to do a chore. Now I know you're up to something."

He left the bedroom and missed the guilty looks his

three children gave each other before following him down-stairs for dinner.

After dinner, Archie headed back to school and Pen de-cided to check out SPYder. Mariana still hadn't confessed to sending the message to SPYder, but maybe there was a lot Mariana wasn't confessing. Pen shut the door to her room, opened up her laptop and maneuvered through her secret file folder to find SPYder. Two more messages waited for her. Pen opened the first one.

Help! I think the girl I like will never feel the same about me. How can I get her to notice me?

Pen rolled her eyes, but she was determined to answer all inquiries. Still, she was glad Quin wasn't here to read this one and laugh at her. She typed:

Your question isn't about if this girl likes you, but if you like yourself. If you like yourself, you'll be yourself and if the girl likes that, she'll like you.

Pen allowed herself a self-satisfied smile. Kostas, her philosophical Greek tutor, couldn't have come up with a better answer. The last question waited in SPYder's inbox. Pen clicked open the text message.

SPYder, my family is being torn apart and I don't know what to do. Can you help me?

Pen caught her breath. Was this Mariana finally decid-ing to come clean and tell Pen everything? It had to be. Pen thought hard and slowly tapped on the keyboard.

If you're in trouble, find people you can trust and ask for help. They will, if you only ask.

Pen sat back and studied the reply. Her own words sank deep into her thoughts. Who did she trust? Not Mariana. She trusted Mamá and Dad, but she couldn't tell them about Mariana and the trophy or they would halt the in-vestigation. She trusted Kostas and her grandparents, but they weren't here.

That left Quin and Archie. The three of them could figure out where the stolen trophy was and who was threatening Mariana's family. She'd tucked the note hidden in
Quin's soccer ball in her desk drawer. She pulled it out and
read it again.

Stay away from Mariana and her family or you'll lose
more than your soccer ball.

There was a clue in here to the entire mystery, Pen felt
sure of it. She just had to know where to look.

$$\mathcal{Q}$$

Quin slipped into his art studio after dinner. The sun had
set but a hint of light still lingered. He stared out the windows at indigo sky, searching for the first star of the eve-
ning. He felt as antsy as he did before a soccer game. Too
bad the next game wasn't until Thursday, the opening day
of the tournament. Quin turned away from the night sky
to the faceless Salvatore Cienfuegos painting. The photo
he'd seen at Mariana's stuck in his head. He picked up a
pencil and quickly sketched in the face from memory. The
keeper now grinned as he stretched out to catch the ball
before it could cross the goal line. Quin nodded. That was
just how Salvatore would defend his goal. With confidence. Quin could do the same in the tournament.

He checked his watch. It was still early and Quin didn't
want to run into Pen again tonight. He didn't want his twin
to grill him anymore on why he wasn't going with her to
meet Mariana tomorrow.

He needed to empty his mind, to let his hands work, so
if something about the golden ball was hidden inside his
head, it could come out. This tended to be the way things
worked for Quin, which was why he loved art. Quin didn't
want to paint another Aztec warrior, though, and now that
he'd sketched in Cienfuegos' face, that painting was practically finished.

His gaze fell across the sketch of the Ballon d'Or. Quin
imagined what it would be like to hold the trophy and feel

the smooth gold and the engraving of letters across its face. Then inspiration struck. He hurried to the bottom desk drawer and pulled out a box of modeling clay Pen had given him for Christmas. Quin hadn't had the time, or the motivation, to use it yet. Now his fingers trembled as he opened the package.

He thrust his hands into the clay and squeezed. It squished between his fingers like day old mud. He kept kneading the clay until he could roll it with ease. He began to round the mound in his hands, rolling it against the desk top and patiently pressing out the lumps. He was totally focused on the work, but his subconscious began to work on the mystery. First he thought about Mariana not wanting to call the police. She was frightened for her family and for Luca. Quin knew what that felt like. He had only to remember having a gun pointed at him after falling out of a tree in Spain.

He flipped the clay over and worked on a rough spot. Then he thought about the man in black and the way he'd turned up at Mariana's soccer game. When he approached Mariana, she hadn't screamed or run away. And then there were the pictures. Quin had spotted the man in black in the picture of Salvatore Cienfuegos and Luca. Who would be at Mariana's soccer game and also at an event with Luca and some of the most famous players in the world? Who would know Mariana's father?

Quin finished rolling the clay and carefully scrutinized it. It was perfectly round and the size of a miniature soccer ball. He picked up a pin tool, shaped like an ink pen but with a steel point, and began etching the polygons.

A knock on the door pulled Quin out of his reverie. He set the pin tool down and looked at his watch. It was almost eleven. Late, even for a Saturday night. He expected Mamá to be at the door, reminding him to go to bed. Instead, Pen walked in. When she saw the clay soccer ball, her eyes lit up. She studied it without speaking and then smiled at Quin. "You just need some gold paint and it'll look like the trophy.

Quin smiled back. "I think I have some of that."

"Listen, I've been thinking about Mariana, and I'm sure there's something she's not telling us. Whatever it is, it's the key to our mystery. Won't you come with me tomorrow and try to find out?" She reached out toward the clay ball.

Quin shook his head. "I can't, but I don't have to. I already know what Mariana's hiding." He gently pushed his sister's fingers away from the clay. "It's still wet."

Pen nodded and tucked her hands under her arms. "Okay, Quintus, I give up. What is Mariana hiding?"

"Mariana and her father know the man in black, and he must be someone important in the soccer world, too, or he wouldn't be in the picture with Luca and Cienfuegos."

Pen shrugged and frowned, a crease in her forehead. It drove her crazy when Quin reached things before she did. "So? Don't we already know that?"

Quin had to smile. "So that means he's probably a Brazilian coach or maybe even an administrator. That means he might be the one who forced Mariana's father to throw those soccer games."

"If he was forced."

"If," Quin agreed, "but if he is..." He paused because this second part both confused him and made him uneasy. "Then who's the man in black working for?"

13

Quin worried all Sunday morning Pen would ask about his afternoon plans, but his sister seemed to have other things on her mind. She grilled Quin in a whisper at breakfast.

"Why wouldn't Mariana tell us about the man in black?" They sat at the kitchen table eating Dad's famous pumpkin pancakes. Their father flipped pancakes at the stove while listening to talk radio. Mamá hadn't emerged yet. When the twins finally left Quin's art studio after midnight, they'd noticed a light still on in Mamá's office.

"Why would she?" Quin mumbled back, his mouth full of pancake and syrup. "Mariana doesn't trust us." He sighed. He couldn't blame someone for not trusting Pen, not that his sister was such an untrustworthy person. But sometimes she let her own ideas get in the way of how she treated others. Quin had always tried to treat everyone as he wanted to be treated, the golden rule Grandma Grey often repeated during their infrequent visits.

Pen frowned and tore into her last bite, chewing furiously. Quin understood his twin's confusion. It didn't make sense that Mariana would ask for their help and not include information vital to their search for the golden ball, but he hadn't been able to focus much on their current mystery this morning. His phone conversation with Anna kept coming back to him. Had he sounded like a complete moron or only half a moron?

Pen's fork clattered onto her empty plate. "Oh," she gasped. "I get it."

"What?" Pen looked like she'd just solved a tough math problem, both triumphant and frazzled.

"More pancakes," Dad called cheerfully. Without waiting for a response, he deposited two steaming pancakes on each plate. "*Dónde está tu mamá*? The way you two are chowing down, she's going to miss out on breakfast."

"Maybe you should wake her up," Pen suggested helpfully.

Dad nodded. "Watch those pancakes on the griddle for me, Penpal, and I will."

Pen scooted her chair back and took up the spatula. Once Dad disappeared down the hall, Quin jumped up from his chair. "I can't stand it. What do you know about Mariana?"

Pen slid the spatula underneath the pancakes and managed to flip them without destroying the perfect circles. She set the spatula down. "I can only think of one reason Mariana didn't tell us her father knows the man in black. Her father must be involved in stealing the Ballon d'Or."

Quin gaped at his twin. "You think Mariana's father is a thief? But that's..."

"*Loco*?" Pen finished. "Isn't stealing the trophy crazy, too? And if the man in black knows Mariana's father, I bet you a hundred pumpkin pancakes he's involved in the missing trophy."

"You're suggesting Mariana's father stole his own brother's trophy?" Quin took off his glasses so the world wasn't quite so clear. It helped him think better. Still, he couldn't imagine stealing anything of Pen's or Archie's, no matter how mad he was at them, and then threatening his own family.

"It doesn't make sense." Quin put his glasses back on. "What about the threat to Luca's family? Would Mariana's father do that?"

"What about ignoring us when we told him about the man on the fire escape?" Pen countered.

Quin sighed. "Well, if Mariana's father is involved, who left the note in my soccer ball?"

Pen shook her head. "I don't know. I'm going to show it to Mariana today."

"Do I smell pancakes burning?" Dad hollered down the hall.

"Oops." Pen scooped the pancakes off the griddle and slid them over on a plate, four perfectly black circles. Mamá walked into the kitchen in her robe, long hair disheveled.

"*Buenos días,*" she murmured, stifling a yawn.

Pen held out the plate of burnt pancakes. "*Buenos días?*"

Quin shook his head and Dad looked aghast. "Pen, when I asked you to watch the pancakes, I didn't mean—"

But Mamá took the plate and kissed Pen on the cheek. "Gracias, *hija.*"

Pen picked up her own plate and slid two of the burned pancakes onto it, sharing the burden. Mamá took a bite, grimaced, and added more syrup to her pancakes. "*Y qué hacen hoy*? Studying?"

Pen groaned. "School just started. We can't spend a whole Sunday studying."

Quin cleared his throat. "Actually, I'm meeting, uh, a study group this afternoon to work on our project for Mr. Hardy's class."

"Who?" Pen narrowed her eyes at him and twirled a pancake in syrup.

Quin shrugged and became very involved in cutting his pancakes.

"*Y tú, m'ija?*" Mamá asked Pen.

"*Nada mucho,* Mamá. I'm going to kick the ball around with Michael at the park. And I think I'll stop by Mariana's and invite her."

"*Qué maravilloso,* you have a new friend, but don't you have a school project, too?"

"Actually, Mariana is my partner for my project, so this gives us a good chance to talk it over." Pen took a huge bite of blackened pancake and chewed furiously. Quin rolled his eyes, but only for Pen to see. He could imagine what kinds of questions his sister would have for Mariana, and it probably wouldn't involve the American Revolution. Still, it would keep her busy while he met Anna.

Dad set a plate of fresh pancakes on the table. "Seconds or thirds?"

"Yes," Mamá said. "And your afternoon plans will have to wait until after church. Go get ready."

The twins sighed. Even a good mystery had to wait until after church.

$$\mathcal{Q}$$

Quin decided to catch the bus down the hill that afternoon so he wouldn't arrive sweaty to D'lite Donuts. Unfortunately, his sister had the same idea. She wanted to ride to Mariana's then backtrack to the park. They rode down, Pen with an old soccer ball under her arm and dressed in soccer shorts and her national team replica jersey. She might have even brushed her hair before putting it into a long ponytail. Quin didn't ask, though. He had his backpack full of schoolbooks and a sketchpad slung over his shoulder.

"Are you going to a study group or the Fall Fest?" Pen surveyed Quin's khaki pants and polo.

Quin's ears flamed but he shrugged. "I didn't do my laundry yet." He knew his twin couldn't say anything back to that. He'd seen the pile of dirty clothes on her bedroom floor that morning.

Pen eyed his clothes and frowned. "Just make sure you're thinking about the mystery some while you're studying. Maybe we can figure out how the man in black and Mariana's father stole the trophy."

"You're running with the theory it was her father?" Quin glanced around to make sure no one was listening, but the Sunday bus crowd was light. An older woman sat a few rows ahead of them and a man who smelled like an old bologna sandwich muttered to himself in the back. Quin wrinkled his nose. "He's our best suspect so far. Our only suspect," she added with a frown. Quin shook his head.

"What I don't understand is where the trophy is now. If Mariana's father helped steal it, why is the man in black even here?"

Pen's face darkened and she pursed her lips. "I don't know," she mumbled. Then her face brightened as the bus pulled to a stop. "But I'm going to find out more today."

"Be careful," he cautioned as she got up to exit the bus, knowing the words would be lost on his sister. She hesitated. "You're not getting off here?"

Quin shook his head. "Next stop. We're meeting at D'lite Donuts." He hoped again she wouldn't ask who he meant by 'we'.

Pen's face brightened. "Can you pick up a bag of chocolate doughboys for me?" She leaped down the steps without waiting for a reply.

He sighed with relief. Buying his sister donuts instead of explaining who he was meeting was getting off easy. He got off at the next stop and walked a quick block to the donut shop. Anna waited for him at a corner table for two.

"Hey."

"Hey." Anna wore a pink shirt that made her hair redder. She'd brushed it out instead of the braid she usually wore to school.

Quin cleared his throat. "So, should we talk about what we want to do for the project?"

"Let's get donuts first."

Quin felt relieved. At least they wouldn't have to talk if their mouths were full.

When Pen knocked on Mariana's door, she heard the deadbolt slide back, then the door cracked and an eyeball peered out. "*Sim*?" Senhora da Silva said. She didn't open the door any wider.

"Can Mariana come to the park and play soccer?"

The eyeball regarded Pen closely. She thought about the threat to Mariana's family. If Luca involved the police, his family would be in danger. Had Mariana told her mother about seeing the man on the fire escape? Pen knew if Mamá thought she or Quin was in trouble, they'd be under house arrest. After a long minute, the door shut. Pen turned to go, but then it opened wide and Mariana walked out. She had her long hair pulled back and wore a Santos T-shirt and red soccer shorts, the most casual Pen had seen her outside of soccer practice.

"*Tem cuidado*," Senhora da Silva called after her, an expression Pen easily understood from her Spanish. Be careful. "*Uma hora, não mais*."

"*Sim*, Mamãe." Mariana shut the door quickly. "I only have an hour."

"I heard." Pen glanced down the hall but they were the only people there. "Did you tell your mom about the man we chased up the fire escape?"

Mariana shot Pen a look of disbelief. "No. If she knew, she'd never let me leave again." The girls headed for the stairs.

"So your father didn't say anything, either?"

Mariana frowned and shrugged. "He says she has enough worry in her mind. What did your brother find?" The girls stepped out the door into bright September sunshine.

Pen shook her head. "Nothing, yet." She felt guilty for not telling Mariana about the notice Archie found on the deep web. "Where's your father?"

"With the Santos. They arrived today."

"I'm surprised you're not with them," Pen said without thinking.

Mariana gave her a dark look. "The Santos are not my team, and my father is not my coach." She stopped abruptly and faced Pen. "Why are you asking questions about my father?"

Pen felt her cheeks flush. "It's just, when Archie was looking for information on the trophy, he found some articles on your father about throwing some games..." She trailed off, unsure how to continue.

Mariana spun away and hurried down the street. Pen switched into a jog to keep up.

"What does that have to do with the Ballon d'Or?" Mariana said harshly.

Pen shook her head. "Maybe nothing. But if you want to solve a mystery, you have to think about all the possibilities. What if someone's still mad at your dad for throwing those soccer games back in Brazil?"

Mariana stopped in the middle of the sidewalk and Pen drew up before she ran into the girl. It occurred to her the Brazilian girl could punch her if she wanted to, and she certainly looked like she wanted to.

"My father didn't do it. Whatever those newspaper articles say." Mariana waved at the air as if to erase words.

"Okay," Pen said before Mariana could turn away. "But why didn't he want to tell the police about the man on the fire escape?"

Mariana bit her lip and looked as vulnerable as she had the first day of school. "I don't know," she whispered.

Pen pulled out the note from Quin's soccer ball and shoved it at Mariana. "Why is someone warning us not to be around you? Do you know who wrote this?"

Mariana scanned it. Her mouth dropped open. She scanned the street. Warily, Pen did the same. "What's going on? Is someone following you?"

"Hey, *chicas*. Let's go," Michael shouted, walking up the sidewalk from the other direction. Pen shoved the note back into her pocket.

"I don't know who that's from," Mariana whispered. "I asked you to help find the Ballon d'Or, not accuse my family of stealing it. Maybe you should do what the note says and stay away from me."

"Last one to the field has to be the keeper," Michael shouted. He took off running and Mariana followed, catching up quickly.

Pen stood still, stung by Mariana's words. She had to ask those tough questions, didn't she? She thought about what she'd read last night while researching spies. Some spies had to play both sides so they could gain the information they needed to win the war. Pen wanted to believe Mariana's father wasn't involved in stealing the trophy, but shouldn't she also find out the truth?

The back of her neck prickled. Pen whirled around and examined the street behind her. About ten feet away, a hedge of bushes bordering the park waved slightly. It's the wind, she told herself, feeling the warm breeze on her cheek. She took a few steps toward the bushes, trying to peer beneath their thick foliage, then stopped. What if she looked under the bushes and someone actually was spying on her? Then what? Pen shivered and wished Quin hadn't ditched her for a study group. How was she supposed to solve this mystery without her partner?

"Hey, Penhead," Michael's voice called to her. He and Mariana had entered the park and were obscured by the hedges along the street. "Are you coming or is it just me and Mariana today?"

Pen gritted her teeth. "That'll never happen," she vowed and dashed into the park.

Quin sucked on his soda straw until it rattled against the cup. He and Anna had discussed the group project and divided the labor. Quin would paint his own piece of revolutionary art as part of the presentation while Anna wrote a poem. Michael could present their project to the class, since neither Anna nor Quin wanted to talk in front of everyone. He couldn't even seem to talk in front of one girl. Anna kept throwing him glances while she made notes. His own notebook was full of quick sketches he'd made while they brainstormed. Quin took another sip from the straw and came up with air.

"Think I'll get a refill." He stood up and hurried to the soda fountain, glad for the distraction. He didn't think meeting a girl would be this much work, especially one he'd known since Kindergarten. He hadn't even found a way to bring up the Fall Fest dance yet. At this rate, he wouldn't ask her until well into next year.

He mixed several kinds of soda together to create his own flavor, sort of like he blended paints. When the cup was full, Quin put the lid on and took a deep breath. He'd found a 400-year-old painted book over the summer and avoided getting killed by an art thief. Surely he could ask a girl to a dance?

When he turned around, Anna was talking to someone at the table, a tall man wearing a dark blue Red Sox cap which covered his head, except for a few freckles on the back of his neck. Quin frowned and walked back, taking a long drink from his soda. Anna glanced his way and the man walked off and out the door without turning around.

"Who was that?"

Anna shrugged. Her face seemed paler than usual. "I don't know. He said he liked your artwork. She pointed to Quin's open notebook. He glanced at the page full of mindless doodling. A picture of the Ballon d'Or. One of Salvatore Cienfuegos and, to Quin's horror, a likeness of the picture Mariana had of Luca and Salvatore at the fundraiser, complete with bowties. Quin swallowed hard. What was he thinking sketching valuable clues out in public for anyone to see? He glanced at the door, but the stranger was gone.

"He left you a note." Anna handed a folded D'lite donuts napkin to Quin. "I read it," she admitted, her face turning the same shade of pink as her shirt. Quin scanned the napkin.

I know you're looking for the golden ball. Stay away

from the tournament or you'll get hurt. All of you.

Quin's mouth had gone dry but he'd forgotten about the soda still in his other hand.

"What did the man look like?" he whispered.

Anna shook her head. "He was here and gone so quickly. What does the note mean? "

Quin shoved the napkin in his pocket, wishing he hadn't lost his phone so he could call Pen. "It means we have to go. Can I borrow your phone?"

14

"Let's take a break," Pen suggested after another shot whizzed by her head into the goal. She was tired of trying to field Michael and Mariana's shots, but even more tired of the way they joked with each other. In fact, this afternoon was turning out to be a bust. As she walked out of the goal, the next shot bounced off her hip.

"Nice save," Michael shouted. Pen rolled her eyes and picked up her phone from the park bench. She had two texts, the first from Archie.

a: I found the IP address! Meet me at St. Mary's. 1 hour.

Pen checked her watch. Archie had sent the text over thirty minutes ago. How long had she been in the goal?

"Come on, Pen," Michael shouted. "I'll switch you. I bet you and Mariana can't score on me."

"Don't count on it," Pen shot back. She quickly checked the next text. It was from Anna.

Don't leave the park. We'll be there soon.

Pen frowned. She didn't remember telling Anna she was at the park. And who was we? It didn't matter. She had about fifteen minutes before she had to meet Archie. Pen jogged out to the field and measured up the goal. Michael waved both arms up and down and wiggled around. "I bet you shoot it right at me," he shouted. Mariana walked over to Pen.

"Kick it at his head." She smirked. Pen decided she liked Mariana and Michael a lot more when they weren't together. She nodded and charged the ball, shooting a rocket straight at Michael. He yelped and ducked. The ball hit the back of the net.

"Penelope!"

"It was an accident."

Mariana giggled and Pen joined in, glad Mariana didn't seem to be angry with her anymore. Then she spotted Anna jogging across the field with her twin.

"What are you two doing here?" Pen asked when they raced up. Both were out of breath. Anna took deep gulps of air. "And what are you doing together?"

She wheeled toward Quin. "I thought you were at a study group. Don't tell me. This is your group? You and Anna?"

Quin looked sheepish. "And Michael, but we decided we might get more done if he didn't come to the meeting." Michael hopped on one foot across the goal line. He waved at them, switched feet and hopped the other way. "Did you finish the project?" he shouted.

"Sorry, Pen," Anna quickly apologized. "We were studying and—"

"Never mind." Quin pulled the napkin out of his pocket. "A man gave Anna this while we were there."

Pen glanced down. "A D'lite Donut napkin?"

"It's what's on the napkin," Quin said.

She scanned the note. "Who gave you this?"

Quin quickly explained how the man had dropped the note with Anna while he refilled his soda.

"Do you think it's from," she glanced at Mariana, still shooting on Michael, and lowered her voice, "the man in black?"

Her twin nodded. "It has to be. Who else? And did you read the part about the tournament?"

Pen held in a shudder. She found that part of the note

particularly chilling. "Why the tournament? What's going to happen there?"

"What's going on?" Anna asked. "Are you two in trouble?" Pen hadn't told Anna too much about their adventure over the summer, but she'd dropped hints here and there.

The twins ignored her. "If he gave you that note in the donut shop," Pen started.

Quin finished. "He followed me there."

"I thought someone was following me, too." She looked around, but the park was full on a beautiful Sunday afternoon. Anyone could be watching them.

"Maybe we should tell Mariana about this," Quin said.

"Later. We're supposed to meet Archie now."

"What? Where?" He looked around as if their older brother might materialize out of the air like a genie.

Pen shook her head. "Not here." For some reason, she didn't want Anna to know where they were going. Anna was her best friend, but she'd met with Quin behind her back. And Anna wasn't a part of this mystery.

"Is anyone going to tell me what's happening?" Anna stomped her foot.

"No," the twins said at the same time.

"I mean," Quin amended, "We can't right now—"

"It's kind of sensitive," Pen added. "We can't tell everyone."

Anna glowered at them. "Oh, you mean you can tell Mariana, a girl you barely know, and not your best friend?"

"Anna, it's not like that," Pen said.

Anna shook her head. "No, it's exactly like that. Since Mariana showed up, you've hardly paid any more attention to me than to Eileen Esposito. I guess you have Quin and Michael and Mariana now. You don't need me."

She turned to Quin and said icily, "See you in class." Then Anna stomped away across the field.

"Wait—" Quin said, but Pen grabbed his arm. "Forget it. She'll get over it. She always does."

He shook his head. "I don't think so. That was kind of—"

but he stopped when Pen glared at him.

"Why do you care anyway? Were you going to ask her to Fall Fest?"

Quin's face flushed a deep red and Pen stared, amazed. "You were?" She couldn't believe it. She'd never given much thought to Quin asking anyone to the dance, let alone her best friend.

"It doesn't matter. She wouldn't go with me now."

He stalked over to Michael and Mariana and Pen heard him making up an excuse to leave. She didn't like the idea of leaving the Brazilian girl here alone with Michael, but they couldn't take Mariana with them, either. Quin headed her direction, his face still taut. Pen wasn't sure what to think of her brother and Anna going to the dance together. But she would have to work on that problem later. The mystery awaited.

$$\rho$$

Archie sat on the front steps of St. Mary's when the twins arrived. "I forgot it's Sunday," he said glumly. "We can't get inside."

"Why would we want to?" Quin examined the empty windows. St. Mary's was the last place he'd choose to be on a weekend.

"What's going on?" Pen took a seat next to Archie. "Why are we meeting here?" Quin leaned against the stair railing.

"I tracked the IP address for the note sent on the deep web."

Pen shook her head. "How? You can track those, but only to their servers. They're supposed to be private."

"What are we talking about?" Quin interrupted, annoyed he didn't seem to understand the significance of the conversation.

"Sorry," Archie said. "IP addresses are those series of numbers attached to any communication on the web. It traces back to where the communication originated but—

"

"But it can only tell you the general area," Pen finished. "It won't give you a name."

"Correct," Archie agreed, "But going to school at MIT has its advantages. I was able to trace the address to the service provider and they helped me track it to here. Whoever sent the message about the trophy sent it from right here inside St. Mary's."

Quin felt like he'd been knocked to the ground in a game. He leaned back against the stair railing to steady himself. "But the only people who use the computers here are teachers and students."

Quin fell silent at his own words and for once, Pen did, too. The twins stared at each other, horrified. Quin saw St. Mary's with new eyes. Each dark window seemed like a sinister eye. What if someone was watching them from inside the school? The same someone who used a school computer to set up the theft of the Ballon d'Or? He could feel the wadded-up napkin in his pocket, the words warning them away from the trophy and the tournament.

"Who could have sent the email from here?" he asked.

Archie shook his head. "The IP address can't tell us that. That's where you come in." He bit his lip and tucked his hands into his black jeans' pockets. "I hate to say this, but I think you both need to investigate a little more."

Pen let out a short squeal and hugged Archie so hard he stumbled back and sat down on the cement steps. "Okay, okay." He laughed, pushing his sister away. Then he grew serious. "But be careful. If you notice anything suspicious, tell me."

Quin felt like the note was burning a hole in his pocket. He started to tell Archie about it, but Pen jumped in.

"We will," she said. "Thanks, Archie. Now, we need to make a list of who at St. Mary's could have sent that message."

"It could be anyone," Quin said, but he had a hard time believing anyone at his school could be involved in this theft.

"Right," Pen said, beaming. "But let's follow the clues. Why was the message about the trophy sent from here? Why not Brazil where Luca is from? Or Spain, where he plays soccer? And if the message was sent from here, wouldn't it mean the trophy was here, too?"

"Let's focus on what we do know, which is that someone sent a message from here advertising for thieves to steal the trophy," Archie said.

"And it was sent around the same time Mariana moved here a few weeks ago," Pen added. "It can't be a coincidence."

"It doesn't seem likely," Archie agreed.

"You mean you both think Mariana has something to do with the missing trophy?" Quin asked.

"She's inside St. Mary's every day," his twin said.

"So's Sister Doris," Quin said. "That doesn't make her the thief."

"It doesn't *not* make her the thief."

"But that doesn't make sense. She's the one who asked us to help find the trophy. Luca is her uncle. Why would she steal from him?" Quin tried to keep the anger he felt from boiling over. Why was his sister so determined to make Mariana the thief?

"Why would she ask us unless she thought it was here?" Pen countered. "We hardly know her, and she's not telling us the truth about everything. She didn't tell us who the man in black was or why he was trying to take her from the soccer game."

"It doesn't mean she knows anything about the trophy."

"Hey," Archie said, holding both hands up as if to squelch the argument. "Unfortunately, that's the end of the road as far as clues go. We don't have much evidence the trophy is here or if Mariana is involved." He looked back and forth at his siblings. "Unless there are things you're not telling me."

Quin fingered the note again. Pen frowned at him and

shook her head slightly. He sighed and took his hand from his pocket. For now they would keep the D'lite Donut napkin a secret. He wasn't sure what the note meant or who had delivered it. No need to alarm Archie yet.

Suddenly the front door opened and Sister Doris emerged, or someone who looked like her, but dressed in jeans and a light pink shirt. She wore a white cap clipped to the back of her head and grey hair poked out in surprising waves. Quin gaped. He'd never seen the head of St. Mary's out of her habit.

"Well, this is a surprise," Sister Doris said as the door locked behind her with a solid click. "The three Grey Reyes siblings at St. Mary's on a Sunday. How are you, Archelaus?"

Archie gave Sister Doris his famous grin. "Just fine, Sister. And yourself?"

"Hmm," the principal said. "Right as rain." She stepped down the stairs to the sidewalk. In her street clothes, Sister Doris seemed less intimidating than when she stalked the halls in her black habit and veil. In fact, Quin thought, she reminded him of Grandmother Grey.

"Now why are you three loitering outside my school?"

"I just miss St. Mary's so much I dragged these two down to see it," Archie said with a deep sigh. He gazed appreciatively at the school building.

Sister Doris made a sound deep in her throat. "I see. And how is MIT faring? Is it challenging you, or are you challenging them?"

"Sister," Pen jumped in. "Why are you here on a Sunday?" She peered at the nun and seemed to be restraining herself from asking the question Quin wanted to know: why wasn't she wearing her habit?

"Why, Penelope Grey Reyes, do you think teachers and administrators only work at school when students are there?"

Pen shrugged. "I guess I never thought about it much."

Sister Doris sighed. "There is much to be done in a

school that can hardly be accomplished when its students are running through the halls."

By now, Quin had picked up on what his sister was after. "So you're not the only one in St. Mary's after school? And on the weekends?"

"Heaven's no. Many of the teachers stay late and come in on weekends to finish their work." Her eyes flicked to Quin. "Or didn't you know your teachers are so dedicated to giving you a fine education?"

"Uh, yes," he stammered.

"Do you mean there are people inside St. Mary's nearly all the time?" Pen's voice crept up an octave and she bounced on her toes.

Sister Doris laughed. "Enough of the time. And the night janitor works late as well." She stopped laughing and examined the three of them. "Why the once over? What are you three up to?"

"Nothing," Quin said.

"Reminiscing about my time here," Archie answered at the same time.

"Research for my American Revolution project," Pen added.

"Mmm," Sister Doris said, managing to convey her doubt in one sound. Quin felt heat spread from his face all the way down to his toes. Sister Doris could smell a lie like Quin could smell Abuela's tacos from half a block away.

She sighed. "Seeing as it's the Lord's day, and my day off, I will give you the benefit of the doubt. I'll see you two tomorrow," she told the twins. She shot Archie one more stern gaze. "Do keep MIT on their toes." Her gaze softened and one eye nearly winked, or perhaps it was just a twitch.

Archie grinned and saluted. The three watched Sister Doris stride down to the bus stop.

"Did you hear that?" Pen asked. "The teachers stay after school and come in on weekends. Any one of them could have sent the email from the school."

"How will we ever find out who did it?" Quin asked. The

thought that any teacher at St. Mary's could be responsible for a crime chilled him.

"Knowing you two, you'll figure it out," Archie said. "Hey, does Mamá still do leftovers on Sunday nights?" He checked his watch and stretched. "I could eat."

"Me too," Quin said automatically.

"You just had donuts," Pen protested. "And you didn't bring me any doughboys."

"Hey, the D'lite Donuts date? How'd that go?" Archie punched Quin's shoulder.

"You told Archie and not me?" Pen shrieked before Quin could answer.

He calmly adjusted his glasses. "I knew you'd react this way. And it wasn't a date," he stressed to Archie. "It was a study group."

"Study group of two," Pen muttered.

Archie laughed and slung an arm around Quin. "Those are the best kinds of study groups, *hermano*."

15

The next few days passed in a blur of school, soccer practice, and homework. Both Mr. Hardy and Ms. Morgan gave the soccer team the class assignments they would miss while playing in the tournament.

Pen spent her evenings researching spies from the American Revolution. She'd asked Mariana to research it, too, but she doubted the Brazilian girl had the assignment on her mind, which meant Pen would have to do all the work. She sighed. This was why she hated group work. Still, Ms. Morgan had intrigued her with the assignment, and she combed the web, stunned at the number of known spies and the methods they used, from secret ink to coded letters and elaborate signals. Compared to the risks these spies had taken to pass information on to George Washington and help win the Revolution, SPYder seemed like a game.

Pen settled on the Culper Ring, a group of spies who helped George Washington know what was happening in New York and who were never caught. Most of the spies took such care with their identities they weren't revealed to be spies until after their deaths. One spy's identity was never even known. The woman, only referred to as Agent 355, was rumored to have perished in a prison ship off the coast after being captured, but not before she'd proved invaluable to the entire network.

Pen shivered at the woman's demise. She knew being an agent of intrigue could be risky, but reading about the dangers and deaths of these spies brought a new soberness to the idea. Pen took copious notes and got so enthralled, she almost forgot about her own mystery. Almost.

Who could have sent the email about stealing the golden ball from a school computer? This question plagued Pen all day Monday. As she moved from Ms. Morgan's class to art, lunch, back to Ms. Morgan's, and finally to soccer practice, Pen carefully considered each teacher. Most of them she'd known since entering St. Mary's in kindergarten. It seemed impossible to suspect any of the Sisters. Sister Agatha, who taught the youngest students, had been at St. Mary's longer, even than Sister Doris.

As she considered all of her former teachers, she kept drawing a blank. Finally, she was left with the new teachers, Mr. Hardy and Ms. Morgan. She watched Ms. Morgan carefully in class that afternoon. Was it possible either one of the seventh-grade teachers was responsible for the email?

"Impossible," Quin said when she suggested it on their way to practice. "All they care about is teaching and homework and maybe a little about the Friendship Cup. Mr. Hardy asked me today if the team was ready to play its best."

"See, maybe he's interested because he sent the email to have the trophy stolen, and he knows we're playing the Santos and Mariana's dad is going to help coach and..." She trailed off. As she spun out the theory it sounded less and less possible, even to her ears.

"Besides," her twin said as they reached the field and jogged to the center circle to gather with the rest of the Saints, "what are we going to do, walk up and ask teachers if they sent the email?" He shook his head. "There has to be another way."

For the next two hours Coach Sikes ran the team through every drill they knew, plus an extra-long scrimmage. Pen had to forget about finding the email's sender while they practiced harder than ever before.

When the coach finally blew the whistle, the team hustled to the center, but not quite as quickly as usual. Everyone was exhausted.

"How are we going to play Thursday if every practice is like this?" Michael muttered to Pen as they reached the center. She shook her head, too tired and thirsty to answer. Even Mariana looked wiped out, her ponytail disheveled and sweat pouring down her face. Pen didn't even have the energy to revel in how she'd scored more goals than Mariana in practice.

"Saints," Coach Sikes said. "Great practice. I know you're tired, but when we start the tournament, we'll have to play harder than we ever have if we want a shot at winning, or even making it out of the first round."

Heads bobbed up and down. "We got this, Coach," Lyla said. Others echoed her enthusiasm.

"Come ready to practice hard again tomorrow. Wednesday we'll take it easy and talk about our upcoming opponents. I want all of you to do your best this week in school and stay out of trouble. Got it?"

Coach Sikes took his time looking each player in the face. Pen swallowed hard and held her gaze steady when the coach's eyes found hers. He probably wouldn't approve of the twins' investigation. Maybe she should drop the entire thing, she thought while she glanced at her teammates. Then her eyes rested on Mariana's. The girl wasn't paying attention to the team. She'd turned toward the sideline, where a man observed the team from the far corner of the field.

Pen poked her brother and pointed to the corner, but the man had disappeared.

"What?" he mouthed.

Mariana turned back to the team, her face drained of color. Pen hadn't been able to tell if it was the man in black or not. Quin poked her back and lifted his shoulders in a shrug.

"Okay, hands in for our cheer," Coach Sikes said.

"Tell you later," Pen whispered as the team shuffled in closer and put their hands together.

"Friendship Cup on three," Coach Sikes called out. "One-two-three."

"You're insane," Quin said. "Absolutely insane."

They'd just exited the bus and started the hike up the hill to the Grey Reyes Manor. And Pen had just dropped her plan on how to find out who sent the email about stealing the trophy.

"Do you have a better idea?"

Quin snorted. "Any idea would be better than yours."

When she glared at him, he sighed. He didn't have a better idea, or any idea, on how to find out who sent the email. And, though he didn't want to admit it, he didn't want to find the sender.

Seventh grade was proving to be more difficult than sixth, and with homework and the tournament coming up, Quin hardly had time to think about the mystery. Not to mention the shiver that ran down his back when Pen told him she'd spotted someone watching practice again, or when he thought about the note from D'lite Donuts warning them away from the golden ball and the Friendship Cup. He felt sick to his stomach just thinking about it. And now Pen wanted them to hack every computer in the school computer lab to try to track down that email.

"What if whoever sent the email didn't send it from the computer lab? All the teachers have laptops and phones. There are computers in the office, too," Quin pointed out, desperate to poke holes in Pen's plan.

"True. It's a long shot that we find the email, but if we

do, we're one step closer to finding the trophy."

Quin sighed. At least this was Pen's specialty, not his. Whatever she planned on doing in the computer lab, the most he could do would be distracting anyone who might come in while Pen worked.

"Ok, fine," he agreed. "What do I need to do? Talk to Ms. Cruz while you do your thing?" Ms. Cruz ran the computer lab but she loved to talk to the students.

"Actually, I need your help. I won't have time to check every computer."

They'd reached their house and entered the back door. "What?" Quin dropped his school bag on the kitchen table. "I don't know how to do any of that stuff. That's you and Archie and Dad—"

"*Hola,*" a voice called out from the direction of Mamá's office. "Is that *mis hijos* home already?"

Quin was surprised when their mother entered the kitchen. Their parents rarely arrived home before the twins. He glanced at the clock on the stove and realized it was later than he thought.

"You both look exhausted. Hard practice?" She gave each twin a brief peck on the cheek and wrinkled her nose. "Why don't you shower while I get dinner started."

"Thanks, Mamá," Pen said brightly. They headed upstairs.

"Dibs on the first shower," Quin said. Pen shrugged. "Fine. But after dinner I'll show you how to figure out who used the computers in the lab so we'll be ready for tomorrow."

Downstairs, Mamá banged pots and pans with gusto. She wasn't the best cook, but she was enthusiastic about the few times during the week she cooked for the family.

He caught Pen's arm before she entered her room. "Have you thought about what could happen if we get caught? Remember what Coach Sikes said about being on our best behavior? I doubt sneaking into the lab is what he meant."

His twin grinned at him. "We won't be sneaking in. We're simply doing research before school like any other student. Stop worrying so much." She shrugged off his hand and shut the door in his face.

"Easy for you to say," he muttered, heading to his own room. With his stomach in knots, he doubted he'd be able to enjoy dinner at all.

They arrived at St. Mary's early the next morning and headed straight for the computer lab. It opened an hour before classes began so students could work. Quin breathed a sigh of relief when they entered. Ms. Cruz wasn't there. Instead, a sign-in sheet sat on her desk. The twins scrawled their names across it. They had to put which computers they would use. "Just pick one," Pen whispered. She wrote 7 next to her name. Quin shrugged and chose 12.

Pen hurried to the first computer and sat down. "Better get started. We don't know when Ms. Cruz will get here."

Quin headed to the opposite end of the room and sat down. He glanced down the line of computers and was startled to see Anna typing at one between him and Pen. She looked his direction, frowned and went back to her work. Quin thought guiltily of the way he'd treated Anna at the park. She'd probably never talk to him again.

He typed in his username, then pulled out a folded note from his pocket. Inside it, he'd written Pen's detailed instructions on how to find all the users on this computer. He quickly clicked through folders until the list came up. Stunned, Quin scrolled through the usernames, disbelieving how easy it had been.

Students were easy to identify. They all had their names with the letters SMS added to the end. Saint Mary's Student. He searched for anything unusual, but it was simply a long list of student users and the names blended together. When Quin reached the end of the list, he shook his head and moved to the next computer.

Quin accessed the names on the computer, found nothing unusual and moved again. The clock ticked closer to the first bell as he worked his way steadily around the room.

"Anything?" Pen whispered behind him. Quin jumped. He hadn't heard his sister approach.

"Nobody but students. Oh, and Ms. Cruz, of course."

Pen sighed. "Same. I guess the teachers don't use the lab, like you said."

Quin couldn't believe his twin was actually admitting he was right. "Well, keep going," Pen said. "We're almost finished, but hurry up."

Quin didn't need anyone to tell him to work faster. He flew through the names on the list and moved to the computer next to Anna.

"Why are you moving from one computer to another?" she asked.

Quin shifted in the chair and shrugged. "Just helping Pen with a project," he muttered.

She rolled her eyes at the obvious lie. "Whatever."

The first bell chimed. Pen hurried over. "Hi Anna," she said brightly. "I guess we better head to class soon or we'll be late."

Anna gave Pen a measured look. She gathered up her backpack and stood. "Don't you have anything you want to say to me?"

Pen started to frown. Quin jumped in. "We're sorry," he said. "We shouldn't have acted the way we did at the park. It wasn't nice."

Pen flicked hair out of her face, stared at her feet, and finally met Anna's gaze. "Right. I'm sorry, too."

Anna nodded and her face relaxed a little. "That's ok. I know you and Quin are usually up to something. See you at lunch?"

"Of course," Pen said. She shot Quin a look he knew well. It said *do something*.

"Hey, do you uh—have a minute to talk?"

Anna pointed to the clock. "We have two minutes to get to Mr. Hardy's class."

"Right," Quin said. "I meant—" he glanced at Pen. "Maybe we can talk in the hall?"

Anna shouldered her bag and shrugged. Quin jumped up and followed her to the computer lab door. He saw Pen shift to Anna's computer. "What is it?" Anna asked, her tone clipped. Why was she still mad at him when she'd forgiven Pen so easily?

Quin bit his lip. "I really am sorry. I didn't mean to make you mad."

Anna rolled her eyes. "It's fine, Quin. I wasn't that mad." She sighed. "Ok, I was because I know you and Pen are up to something. Pen and I have been friends a long time. But that's not why I was mad."

"Wait, it wasn't?"

Anna shook her long red hair. "No. I'm used to you and Pen doing your twin thing. You've always had this way of shutting out the rest of the world sometimes. I mean, I'm jealous of it, but I sort of get it. You're twins."

"Oh." Quin didn't know what else to say. No one had ever told him this before. Did he and Pen really shut out the world?

"What I was mad about was—" Anna stopped and her cheeks flamed as red as her hair. "I thought you were going to ask me to the Fall Fest dance and you didn't."

Quin's mouth dropped open. He wanted to tell Anna he was going to ask her, but he couldn't find the words.

"But then I realized I was being silly waiting around for you to ask me," Anna continued. "So, I'm asking you. Do you want to go to the Fall Fest dance with me, Quintus Grey Reyes?"

Quin nodded, then realized he should say something. "Yeah. Sure."

The door to the lab opened, banging him in the back. "Ow."

"Sorry," Pen said. "I thought you already left for Mr. Hardy's. Uh, Anna, can I talk to Quin alone?"

"See," Anna whispered to Quin and poked his arm. "Twin thing." She walked away.

"I knew she wouldn't stay mad for long," Pen said.

"That's not why—" Quin started to say, but she cut him off.

"I found something on the last computer."

"Hello, Pen and Quin," Ms. Cruz approached them with a cup of coffee and her usual smile. "Shouldn't you two be headed for class?"

Pen tugged him down the hall and waved to Ms. Cruz. They hurried down the nearly empty hall to the seventh-grade classrooms.

"So someone who wasn't a student used the computer? Who?"

Pen shook her head. "No, it was a student." They stopped at the door to Mr. Hardy's room. "I found Mariana's username."

"So what? Almost every student in St. Mary's has probably used the lab at some point."

"But she's new. And the date she accessed the computer was two days before school started and," his sister paused dramatically, "the day before the Ballon d'Or was stolen."

Quin let this sink in. It was strange Mariana had used the lab before school started. "So you think Mariana sent that email? How would she know how to do that? Archie said he found it on the deep web. It was supposed to stay hidden."

"I don't know," Pen admitted. "All I know is, something doesn't add up in this mystery."

16

It felt strange to arrive at St. Mary's the morning of the Friendship Cup in their blue and white Saints warm-ups, carrying gym bags full of gear and uniforms. Sister Doris insisted on holding a pep rally for the team, an unusual occurrence at St. Mary's. The other students cast jealous looks as they filed into the school gym for the assembly.

Sister Doris opened the assembly by speaking on sportsmanship and the privilege of being invited to play in the tournament. Pen half listened, wondering if the principal had ever played sports in her life. The picture in her head of the principal in her habit and veil made Pen giggle. She looked around the gym. Most of her teammates fidgeted, hardly able to hold still through the assembly. Even Quin frowned at the long speech and tapped all ten fingers on the bleachers as if his hands itched to catch a soccer ball.

Pen caught Ms. Morgan whispering something to Mr. Hardy behind her hand. Both teachers stifled laughter. Sister Doris suddenly cleared her throat and glared at that part of the room. Pen's eyebrows rose. Even teachers couldn't concentrate during one of Sister Doris's speeches. Then Pen saw Eileen Esposito staring at her. Eileen's eyes narrowed until they looked like the slits of cat's eyes, mean and cunning.

Pen turned away. She and Eileen hadn't spoken since

she'd knocked the jelly beans out of Eileen's hand, and between the mystery of the golden ball and researching the
Culper Spy Ring, Pen hadn't thought much about Eileen.
She remembered when Eileen had tried to make Anna her
best friend in fifth grade. Anna had been flattered and split
time between the two of them, but when it became clear
Anna wouldn't stop hanging out with Pen, Eileen returned
to snubbing them both. Anna was a loyal friend, Pen reflected. She sighed, feeling bad for the way she'd treated
Anna at the park. Still, why hadn't Anna told her she was
meeting Quin? Did she think Pen would be jealous? Of her
brother? Was she? Pen chewed on her lip. Her phone
buzzed deep in her warm-up pants pocket, making her
jump. Pen squirmed to pull it from her pocket without anyone seeing. The screen showed a new text from Archie.

α: Suspect arrested in Spain for stealing Ballon d'Or.
Mystery solved. Guess we were wrong about the email
sent from St. Mary's.

Pen felt like she'd just watched the game winning goal
slide into her opponent's net. How was this possible? She'd
felt certain the Ballon d'Or and its thief were here in Boston. She hurriedly typed back:

π: Did they find the trophy?

The reply was almost instantaneous, like her question
and Archie's answer had crossed in space.

α: No trophy yet, but the arrest is a good start. So no worries for today's tournament. Buena suerte!

Archie's wish for good luck rolled right off Pen. She
shook her head and tucked the phone away before she got
caught. A hiss got her attention. Quin, sitting on the other
side of Mariana, leaned forward. "What happened?" he
mouthed.

Pen leaned over and whispered Archie's text to him,
which meant Mariana and Michael, on Quin's other side,
also heard. Quin grinned slowly. "Brilliant," he whispered.
"That means it's not..." He stopped. They hadn't told

anyone about Mariana using the computer lab. Pen looked at the Brazilian girl to see how she was taking the news. She sat straighter and her face glowed.

"*Meu familia* is safe," she whispered.

"Fist bump." Michael held his fist out to Mariana. She looked surprised but she bumped it.

"Cut it out," Quin whispered, caught in between the two. "Sister Doris is looking at us."

Sister Doris had finally relinquished the microphone to Coach Sikes. Now she crossed her arms and sent the four of them a stern gaze. The coach started talking about the team's success last season, led by leading scorers Pen Grey Reyes and Michael Blalock.

"Yeah!" Michael leaned over Quin and Mariana to bump fists with Pen.

She blushed. "Stop, or they'll never let us leave."

Michael shook his head and kept his fist out. She sighed and bumped it.

"With a solid performance in goal by Quin Grey Reyes," Coach Sikes continued, beaming at Quin. "We look forward to another amazing season." The students broke into a smattering of applause and Quin's cheeks flushed, but he waved to the room.

"Oh brother," Pen whispered. She glowered at the floor. She should be happy the *policía* had made an arrest. It would probably be only a few hours or days before the trophy turned up as well. But how could the thief still be in Spain, when all the clues they'd found led straight to Boston? Archie's deep web search to the computer lab, the strange man on the fire escape at Mariana's apartment, and Quin's mysterious notes in his soccer ball and at D'lite Donuts. Why would someone warn them away from the tournament if the trophy and its thief were in Spain? It didn't add up.

"And with the addition of Mariana da Silva," Coach Sikes continued, "we expect big things from this little soccer team." He beamed at his players. "Stand up, Saints."

The players shuffled to their feet. In the commotion, Quin slipped past Mariana to stand next to Pen. She noticed Michael immediately started whispering in Mariana's ear, standing on tiptoe to do so.

"What?" Pen realized Quin was talking to her.

"I said, it's awesome the police found the thief."

She shook her head. "But what about the note at D'lite?"

"Maybe someone was trying to scare us so we wouldn't play. One of the other teams' coaches?"

Pen frowned. Would coaches stoop to threatening notes? The only other coach they knew was Mariana's father, and he didn't know the twins were investigating the missing trophy, did he? She was about to mention this when Coach Sikes said, "If we play together, I expect we can win the tournament." The school cheered and clapped. St. Mary's pep squad, led by Eileen Esposito, pranced to the front and started the school cheer.

"But what about—" Pen started, but Quin cut her off.

"Can't we just worry about the tournament? We could win!" She suddenly remembered how he'd worried about his arm all summer. Now he clapped hard with the rest of the team like the bone had never been broken. Maybe Quin was right and she was chasing the wrong trophy.

"Okay," Pen agreed. "Let's get the trophy."

"Yeah," Michael echoed. "Get that trophy."

The team took up the chant, drowning out the pep squad. The rest of the students cheered, too. "Get that trophy. Get that trophy."

Eileen waved her pom poms frantically and tried to focus the students back on the school cheer. Pen smiled. Well, if they couldn't find the Ballon d'Or, the Friendship Cup trophy would do. She made up her mind to forget about the mystery and focus only on the soccer tournament.

By the time the team pulled into the multisport complex

where the tournament would be held, they could hardly contain their excitement. The bus pulled past the football stadium and followed signs to the soccer fields. Banners welcomed the teams to the Friendship Cup and players in uniforms of all colors and designs wandered through the complex.

"Stay together," Coach Sikes barked as they got off the bus. "Our game is on field five and warm-up starts in ten minutes."

While Coach Sikes and a few parent volunteers checked the team in under a huge canopy, the players gazed at the activity around them. Several games were already being played. Quin heard snatches of conversation in English, Spanish, and a language he couldn't identify. Then he tilted his head. The unmistakable lilt of Portuguese drifted through the crowd. Mariana spun around and cried out. A team dressed in black and white stripes headed toward them.

"Santos!" Mariana shouted. Several players rushed forward and Mariana met them with fierce hugs.

"Maybe we should adopt their tradition," Michael said, watching the lean Brazilian boys greet Mariana with kisses on each cheek. Pen punched him in the shoulder.

"Mariana, *venha aqui.*" Mariana's father walked behind the Brazilian team. He wore a black Santos hat. Beneath it, his face was lined and grey.

Mariana meekly greeted her father, then walked over to Coach Sikes. "This is my father, Daniel da Silva."

Coach Sikes stuck out his hand. "Pleased to meet you, but I wish you were coaching the Saints, instead."

Mariana's father frowned. "I only coach teams that can win."

"Papai," Mariana said, "this is my team."

Her father frowned and shook his head. He gestured to the Brazilians in black and white behind them. "You play for the wrong Santos, Mariana."

Mariana took a step back from her father. "This is my

team now. St. Mary's is my school."

Her father nodded curtly. "For now." He surveyed the rest of the Saints. *"Boa sorte."* He sounded like good luck was the last thing he wished for them. He turned back to the Santos and shouted at them in Portuguese.

Mariana crossed her arms and kicked the ground.

"And I thought not having a dad was rough," Michael said. "What a jerk."

"Time to warm up," Coach Sikes called. "Let's show those kids from Houston how tough a bunch of Saints can be."

Quin reached out and tugged on Mariana's arm. The girl lifted her head slightly. Tears threatened to spill over.

"Vamos," Quin said. "Let's win the whole tournament and show your father which Saints are the best."

Mariana hesitated, then hugged Quin. He froze, not sure what to do. Girls didn't hug him. Definitely not beautiful Brazilian girls.

"Thank you for helping me, Quintus Grey Reyes," Mariana whispered. "Even if we don't find the trophy."

Pen stared at them with a bemused expression, as if she could read her brother's thoughts. Michael bounced his soccer ball up and down and glared at Quin. "Hey, break it up, you two," he said. "We have a game to play."

Mariana released him and stepped back, smiling. "Let's go score some goals."

🔍

The Houston Hotshots turned out to be just that. Quin spent the entire game diving after shots on goal that tested his arm and his reflexes. Luckily, the Saints had their own hotshots. With ten minutes left in the first half, the score was tied 3-3, with Pen, Michael, and Mariana each netting a goal for the Saints.

At halftime Coach Sikes told the team if they were tied near the end of the game, he would pull a defender and put in a "power line," as he called it. The defense for each team was determined not to allow more goals and despite several close shots, nothing went in. Quin wasn't surprised when Coach Sikes called for a substitution and pulled Kyle Jenkins out of defense. Pen came into the game after sitting out most of the second half. While the ball was on the other end of the field, Quin had watched her stomping up and down the sideline.

They only had five minutes left. Quin thought of a game he'd watched last spring between Valencia and Atlético. A hotheaded Valencian forward had gotten a red card and been ejected from the match. For the rest of the game, Salvatore Cienfuegos defended his goal against a barrage of attacks, goaltending like Quin had never seen. Quin had been convinced it was this game that put Cienfuegos in the running for the Ballon d'Or, even though Luca had edged him out for the win. Just thinking about Cienfuegos' saves filled Quin with confidence.

For the next five minutes, the Saints gave everything they had. Any time the Hotshots got close to the goal, Quin's defenders cracked the ball away. The midfield ran like crazy to send passes to their three forwards, and Pen, Michael, and Mariana all had close shots on goal. But when the referee blew his whistle, the game was still tied 3-3. Not the greatest start to the tournament. Quin watched his teammates' shoulders sag as they lined up to shake hands. They could still win their next games and make it to the finals, but a tie made things harder.

"Good game, good game," Quin muttered, slapping the Hotshots' palms. He spied a black hat on the Hotshots' sideline. Mariana's father. Figures, Quin thought. He was probably cheering against them.

"Mariana," her father called as they finished greeting the other team. "*Venha cá.*" He pointed to the space in front of him to illustrate his point. The Brazilian girl hesitated.

"Bring it in, Saints," Coach Sikes called. She followed the rest of the Saints to the sidelines to listen to the coach.

"Not bad," Coach Sikes said. "I thought we might get one

in the end, but let's put that down to first game jitters. We still got one point for the tie. If we win our next two games, we'll be fine and move on to the next round."

"Mariana."

Mariana's shoulders stiffened as her father shouted again. Coach Sikes paused and his eyes flicked toward the other sideline. "I want you all to get some rest before our next game this afternoon. It'll be tougher since we'll be tired, but so will the other team. You may—" Coach Sikes stopped and his jaw hardened. Mariana's father stalked toward them, his face red beneath his hat.

"Papai." Mariana's cheeks flamed the same shade of red as her father's.

"You will not win the *torneio* if you play like this. You play *tímida*, not like Luca."

Mariana's eyes fell to the ground. Quin felt anger rush through him. Mariana had worked just as hard as anyone else on the team. Apparently, Pen felt so too. She stepped in front of Mariana. "That's not fair. Mariana took good shots—"

"I am not talking to you," Mariana's father shouted at Pen.

Maybe Quin was still channeling Salvatore Cienfuegos because he planted himself between Mariana's father and her. "You can't talk to my sister like that." He glanced at Mariana, her head lowered. "Or Mariana, either."

Daniel da Silva's face darkened. "Do not tell me what I can do." He poked Quin hard in the chest with his finger. "Or I will—" but Daniel da Silva didn't get to finish his threat.

A tall form brushed past both twins and knocked the finger away. Quin caught his breath. He'd seen *el fuego*, Mamá's quick temper, plenty of times. Pen had inherited the same fire. Mamá seemed to grow taller in her red high heels and leveled her gaze at Daniel da Silva.

"Stop it. These children played hard. It was a good game and you're not going to criticize any of them. Not mine and not yours. Don't you have your own team to boss around? Stay away from ours." Then she repeated everything she'd said in Portuguese, except, Quin thought, with a little extra venom.

Mariana's father looked ready to reply, but Dad, Coach Sikes, and Kyle Jenkins' father stepped closer to the group. Mariana's father's lips tightened as if he wanted to say more but he stepped back. "Good luck with the rest of the tournament. The Santos can't wait to beat you."

The Saints watched Mariana's father walk across the field to where his team waited for their own game, the black hat bobbing with his angry strides.

"Wow," Quin whispered to Pen. "And I thought Mamá could get mad at you."

"*Estás bien, hijo?*" Mamá asked. She wrapped an arm around Quin, then drew Pen in with the other one. "You were right to defend your sister and friend," she whispered so only the twins could hear. "I'm proud of you both."

Dad put a hand on both of their shoulders. "And you played great. Just like Salvatore Cienfuegos."

Quin shot him a surprised look. "I didn't know you followed international soccer."

"How could I not know who my son's hero is?" Dad winked at him. "Besides me, of course."

"Oh, I almost forgot," Mamá said. "We have peanut butter sandwiches and oranges for everyone."

The team cheered and they started for the sidelines. "Hey, where's Mariana?" Michael asked. Pen and Quin looked around. They couldn't find Mariana's highlighted ponytail anywhere.

"I'll look for her," Quin offered, thinking how much he'd hate it if his father had embarrassed him in front of the whole team. Of course, Dad never would. Quin cast a long look at his father, who now passed out sandwiches like it was the most important thing he'd ever done. Beside him, Mamá tossed oranges to Quin's teammates. They'd both taken off work to be at the tournament today.

One orange nearly knocked Coach Sike's cap off. Pen leaned toward Quin's ear. "We're lucky." Quin didn't have to ask what she meant.

"Let's find Mariana," Quin said. "She can't have gone far." They jogged away from field five and scanned the crowd at the next game.

"Hey, wait up." The twins stopped and waited for Michael. He jogged up with a sandwich in one hand and an orange in the other. "I'll come, too," he said, his mouth full of peanut butter.

"Good thing you didn't let your appetite stop you," Pen said.

Michael shrugged. "Gotta refuel. If we don't win the next game, we're toast."

"I know, so we better find Mariana fast." She hesitated, then added, "I'm not sure we can win without her."

Quin couldn't believe his ears. His sister was actually admitting they needed Mariana? But he only nodded. "We're a better team with her."

🔍

They searched around all five soccer fields. At first they stayed together, but when they couldn't find Mariana right way, Michael suggested they split up. He headed for the Santos game currently in progress to see if Mariana happened to be watching her old team. Pen decided to circle the other fields again and Quin returned to the Saints sideline to make sure Mariana hadn't shown up.

Pen slowly wandered through the crowd searching for the Brazilian girl's signature height and blond streaked ponytail. Most of the players in the tournament were boys, so this should have made her job easier, but lots of parents and siblings were there and with other teams crowding the sidelines, waiting for their games, Pen started to doubt they could find Mariana. Why had Mariana's father said such terrible things? Pen remembered the way he'd shut the door in their faces the first time he'd met them, and how he refused to call the police about the man on the fire escape.

She circled the last field and started back, walking slowly. Pen's phone dinged and she pulled it out of her jacket pocket. It was Michael.

Did you find her?

No.

Meet you at the team tent?

Pen hesitated. She knew that's what she should do. Mariana would probably show up after she worked out her anger. Surely she wouldn't miss the next game. Still, Pen wasn't sure, and if she returned to the tent, she'd have to wait and see if Mariana came back, or tell her parents and they would want to get involved. Either way, things would be out of Pen's hands, which is not the way she liked it.

Pen was on the outer edge of the park, near the street. Nobody else was on the gravel pathway which circled all of the fields. She turned back toward the fields, her eyes on her phone. She glanced up in time to catch the flash of a Red Sox cap and a tall man disappearing behind a maintenance shed.

She looked around. A couple of college co-eds jogged slowly down the pathway leading to the Charles River, which wound its way down the other side of the sports complex. A roar from the crowd at the nearest soccer field filled the air. Traffic rolled by on this busy afternoon. The man was probably a spectator waiting for the next game. Or a coach. Or a maintenance worker. Still, Pen felt she'd seen him before.

She walked quickly toward the shed, but her phone buzzed. Pen looked down, expecting a text from Michael asking why she hadn't responded. The alert was from SPYder instead. She pulled up the new text message.

Stop your search for Mariana or you'll be in more danger. Go home and forget the Ballon d'Or.

Pen gasped and stood still while a thousand thoughts swirled inside her head. Who was texting her from SPYder? How did they know about the Ballon d'Or, or that Mariana was missing? How did they even know about SPYder? Only the students from St. Mary's received those texts.

Pen's hands shook as she hastily sent a reply.

Who are you? Where is Mariana?

The phone remained silent in her hand. Pen shook it. "Come on," she muttered. "Give me something." Nothing happened. Pen sighed and checked the time on her phone. Almost time for the second game. If she didn't hurry, she'd be late. Coach Sikes wouldn't like that at all. Neither would her parents.

Her phone beeped again. This time it was Michael.

Where are you? Game in 5. Coach talked to Mariana's dad. He sent her home.

Pen shoved the phone in her jacket pocket and started jogging back to the soccer field. Making Mariana miss the rest of the tournament sounded exactly like something Daniel da Silva would do, but why not tell anyone he'd sent her home? And had Mariana's father sent the text to SPYder? How? She arrived at the sidelines just as Coach Sikes was giving the starting lineup.

"Where have you been, Grey Reyes?" Coach Sikes looked frazzled.

Pen decided to go with the truth. "I was looking for Mariana but I couldn't find her."

"It seems she won't be playing the rest of the tournament with us." He glared over Pen's head to the next field, where the Santos had just finished their game.

"What a jerk," Lyla Thompson said. "Mariana's dad isn't letting her play and he is still coaching the Santos?"

Everyone nodded their agreement.

"Doesn't matter," Coach Sikes said. "We have to think about this game." His eyes landed on Pen. "So Grey Reyes, you're up front with Blalock." He leveled a stern gaze at his team. "Let's show the Santos who the best team is in this tournament."

The Saints cheered and got ready to take the field, but Pen leaned over and showed Quin the text before shoving her phone into her bag. Quin gave her a troubled look, surely thinking the same thing as Pen. Was Mariana really at home or was she in trouble? And who was texting Pen on SPYder?

The team counted to three and shouted "Go Saints" from the huddle before the starters jogged onto the field. Pen took her usual spot next to Michael. These last few weeks all she'd wished for was to have her spot on the field back. Now she'd give anything for Mariana to be here in her place.

17

Luckily, this team wasn't as talented as the last because Mariana's disappearance had Quin rattled. The Saints worked hard for the first half, but neither Pen nor Michael could score and Quin only kept the game scoreless because of the defenders in front of him. At the halftime whistle, Lyla Thompson pulled Quin aside.

"What's going on, Grey Reyes? You acted so scattered in the net I started kicking every ball that came near the goal up the field so you wouldn't have to make a save."

"Yeah, thanks," Quin muttered.

"Hey." Lyla shook him by the shoulders. "Snap out of it. It's bad enough Pen and Michael are playing like zombies up front and Mariana decided to skip the game. She's probably in league with the Santos. I bet she finishes the tournament with them."

"That's not true," Quin snapped. "Her dad made her miss this game."

Lyla shrugged. "If we don't get it together, we'll lose this game and we might as well not even play the last one, we'll be so far behind in points."

Coach Sikes spent halftime encouraging the midfield to shoot more. "If our forwards can't score, our goals have to come from someone else."

Quin barely listened. His mind was too busy wondering

why Daniel da Silva had sent Mariana home, and if he actually had.

"Grey Reyes," Coach Sikes said, pulling Quin back to the team talk. "Do I need to tell Leary to warm up?"

Quin shook his head. Lyla and the other defenders, Kyle Jenkins, Mario Alvarez, and Sean Sullivan, crowded around Quin.

"We've been talking," Lyla said. "Whatever's bothering you, we want you to know, we got this. We're not letting anything get by us."

Quin punched one fist into the glove of his other hand. "Thanks. I'm ready. Let's win this."

The game started again and Quin fought harder to forget what was happening outside of the movement of the ball on the field. He made a brilliant diving save, drawing cheers from the sideline. When he got back to his feet, Michael gave him a thumbs-up from the midline. Quin restarted the game and Michael quickly scored the first goal. Pen scored on a breakaway she tucked neatly into the lower left corner of the net. Then Kevin Chan scored a long shot from his midfield position. When the referee blew the final whistle, the Saints had won 3-0.

As soon as the whistle blew, Quin sprinted off the field, forgoing the usual handshakes with the other team. He reached his parents at the same time as Pen.

"Did you hear from Mariana?" Quin burst out.

Mamá shook her head. "No, *mis hijos*." She frowned. "I'm sorry your friend did not get to play. Some people—" She bit her lip in a way that reminded Quin of his twin.

"Good game," Dad said. Pen grimaced and Quin glared at his father.

"Okay, not your best efforts, but it was enough, and I know you're worried about Mariana."

Mama sighed. "Michael's mother talked to Mariana's father after you couldn't find her. He insisted Mariana was disappointed in how she'd played and chose to go home on her own."

Quin snorted and Pen rolled her eyes. "You mean he was disappointed."

Mamá sighed. *"Tal vez.* But even if we don't agree, he's still her father, and they're in a difficult situation."

The twins stared at their mother. Did she know anything about their investigation into the Ballon d'Or?

"Well, my life wasn't easy when I first moved to this country."

"Oh, right," Quin said, clearly relieved.

"But you had me to help," Dad said with a laugh. Mamá made a noise in her throat, halfway between laughter and disapproval.

"Hey, did I miss it?" Archie hurried up. "The game's over?"

"Nice timing, as usual," Pen said. While her parents laughed, Pen mouthed a silent message to Quin and Archie. "We need to talk."

Quin nodded. That was an understatement. The entire game all he could think about was the text from SPYder. *Stop your search for Mariana.* Quin knew Mariana wouldn't have quit the team so easily, even if her father wanted her to. Her sudden disappearance felt more ominous.

"Here's an idea," Quin said as casually as he could. He tossed his goalkeeper gloves in his bag. "Archie can drive Pen and me home and you two can pick up pizzas on the way."

Mamá and Dad exchanged amused glances. "Are you trying to get us alone, or to get away from us?" Dad responded. His tone felt only half joking.

Quin laughed. It sounded fake to his ears and he quickly stopped. "I just thought pizza sounded good tonight, but I want to shower after playing two games."

Mamá raised her eyebrow, a classic Reyes move. "My son wants to shower before he eats?" She scrutinized Quin. "Are you sure there's something you're not telling us. Perhaps the reason for your sudden interest in personal hygiene?"

Quin started sweating like he was back in the goal. "No."

"Ha," Pen said. "Like you didn't meet Anna yesterday. He wants to ask her to Fall Fest."

Mamá's eyebrow drifted higher. "*Sí?*"

Pen was distracting their parents from the real reason they wanted Archie to take them home, but why had she picked his study date with Anna?

"Michael's going with Mariana." The words were out before Quin could stop them. He regretted it instantly.

Pen froze. She blinked at Quin, then her face clouded over and she shrugged. "So what? Why should I care?" She grabbed her bag and swung it on her shoulder. "*Por favor, Mamá, la pizza?*"

"Okay, okay. Pizza it is."

Dad dropped his arm around Mamá and pulled her closer. "Actually, it's a great idea. We have both been busy lately. It's a date."

"It's only takeout." Pen exaggerated her eye roll. Dad winked at them and kissed Mamá.

"Dad! Mamá!" Quin protested. He hoped none of his teammates had seen such a public display. Fortunately, most of them had grabbed their gear and were heading to the parking lot.

"Ay, *mis hijos.*" Mamá laughed. "*Nos vemos en casa.*" She and Dad walked off, arm in arm.

"I'm glad that's over," Quin said.

"I think it's kind of sweet," Pen said, her eyes on their parents.

"Hey, you two," Archie said. "I'm guessing you have more than pizza on your mind. What is it?"

Pen hurriedly told Archie about the texts she'd received on SPYder. "At first I thought it was another student. Maybe even Mariana. But the last one doesn't sound like anyone from St. Mary's. I don't understand how they know about SPYder or who it could be. Who would want to warn us about the Ballon d'Or?"

Quin was distracted by a crowd forming near the tournament check in table where the tournament trophies were displayed. Kids flocked to the table but he couldn't see why. To view the Friendship Cup trophy the teams could win?

"That programming was secure," Archie said. "I don't see how anyone could have hacked into it. There's only one way someone could be contacting you through SPYder. They must have your original text. The number you sent your classmates for inquiries." Archie gave Pen a stern look that reminded her of their father. "You did only send it to students at St. Mary's, didn't you?"

"Of course," Pen cried.

"And who knows you're looking into the golden ball?"

"Only us and Mariana." Pen bit her lip. "Michael and Anna guessed something, but I don't know what, and Eileen Esposito's been acting weird, but how she could possibly know anything..."

"What's going on over there?" Quin gestured to the check-in table. He was half listening to the conversation.

"It doesn't matter how they got the number," Pen said. "Whoever contacted me knows we're looking for the trophy, however they found out."

Archie shoved a mop of black hair away from his face. "You're right, Penhead. Let's get out of this crowd and back to the house. I don't like that last message you received. The one about being in danger."

"Wait," Quin said. He'd spotted someone at the tent, a man whose movements looked eerily familiar. He pushed through the crowd.

"Quin," Pen protested behind him. "We have to go. We don't have much time before Mamá and Dad get home and I want to stop at Mariana's."

They'd reached the edge of the crowd and broken through to the source of commotion.

"I don't believe it," Quin whispered.

"How? Why's he here?" Pen stammered.

The crowd began to chant two syllables. "Lu-ca. Lu-ca. Lu-ca."

Luca da Silva stood in the center of the crowd, signing anything shoved at him: tournament fliers, soccer balls, jerseys, even shoes. Luca glanced up and Quin caught the green of his eyes, the same eyes as Mariana.

Quin walked forward like his feet had a mind of their own. Luca looked just like the pictures he'd seen at Mariana's. The same hair and eyes as Mariana, and even the same smile that curved pleasantly upward. When Quin reached him, Luca automatically held out his hand for something to sign. When Quin didn't hand him anything, Luca looked up.

"You want me to sign your jersey? he asked, examining Quin's sweaty soccer shirt with a frown.

"Yes," Quin said, without meaning to, and the international soccer star penned his name onto Quin's left shoulder.

"I'm Penelope Grey Reyes, and this is my brother, Quintus," Pen said, stepping up beside Quin. "And we need to talk right now."

Luca cocked his head. "You are Pen and Quin? *Amigos de* Mariana?"

Quin felt his tongue thicken. He swallowed several times and forced it to work. "She told you about us?"

Luca capped the pen in his hand. "*Claro*. The girl who scores goals like me and the boy who stops them like Salvatore Cienfuegos."

"She said that?" Quin stammered.

"Mariana thinks I score like you?" Pen echoed, disbelief in her voice.

"Where is Mariana?" Luca asked. He waved away other requests for an autograph. "I came to see my niece play."

Pen gasped. "So you don't know?"

Luca frowned and focused his green eyes on the twins. "What is there to know?"

"We're not sure where Mariana is," Quin started. "But we think it has to do with your trophy."

Luca's eyes widened. "My Ballon d'Or? What do you mean? And where is Mariana?"

"It's a long story," Pen said.

Quin took Luca by the arm, incredulous he was touching Luca da Silva. Still, Mariana was missing and they were the only ones who could help find her.

"I think you better come with us."

18

Archie drove Pen, Quin, and Luca to Mariana's apartment. On the way, Pen explained how Mariana's father had yelled at her after the game and how Mariana disappeared. She added Daniel da Silva told the team he'd sent Mariana home before their next game. Luca's face grew pensive. Quin sat in silent awe. He couldn't believe Luca was in the car with them. And how normal he looked.

"It does not make sense," Luca said. "Daniel is hard on Mariana, but I do not understand why he would forbid her to play. He loves to watch Mariana play."

"What if he took her," Pen whispered to Quin, but Archie heard.

"Who?" Archie asked.

Pen pressed her lips together. Quin shook his head and answered. "The man who stole the trophy. The one who keeps leaving us notes."

"They arrested someone already," Archie said. "I told you. And I thought you only got one note."

"Ummm," Pen hedged.

"Actually, the police let that man go," Luca said. "He wasn't the thief."

Quin drew a sharp breath. "You mean the trophy's still missing?"

"*Sim*," Luca said. "But what does this have to do with

Daniel and Mariana?"

Archie parallel parked in front of the apartment build-ing. They hurried up the stairs and knocked on Mariana's door. It flew open and Mariana's mother gasped and hugged Luca.

"You're here," she said in Portuguese. "Thank good-ness." She released Luca and looked around the hall. "But where are Daniel and Mariana?"

"She's not here?" Quin asked, stepping into the apart-ment to confirm it. Mariana's mother shook her head.

"Uh-oh," Pen whispered. Mariana's mother stared at the three Grey Reyes siblings. "What's going on?"

"Mariana's missing," Quin said. "And we think," he hes-itated and looked at Pen. She nodded. "We think maybe her father is involved with the missing Ballon d'Or."

Mariana's mother stepped back and put a hand to her mouth like she was holding back a scream. "Is this true, Luca?"

Luca frowned and shook his head. "I'm not sure. I hoped after we left Brazil Daniel wouldn't involve himself in..." He stopped and looked at his sister-in-law. "Maybe we should talk alone."

"But," Pen said, but Archie put a hand on her shoulder.

"Let them go," he whispered. "This isn't your family. And I want to know what other notes you've received. Let's go home."

They clunked downstairs to Archie's car while Quin told their older brother about the note on the D'lite Donut nap-kin warning them away from Mariana. By the time they arrived home and filed into the kitchen, Archie's frown was so deep it reminded Quin of their father.

"I have to tell Mamá and Dad about this. Especially after the trouble you two got into this summer."

"Archie, no," Pen cried. "If you do, our case is over. They probably won't even let us play in the game tomorrow."

"*Lo siento, hermanita,*" Archie apologized. He sighed hard and pushed his hair back with two hands like he wanted to pull it out. "But I have to."

"This isn't fair! Mariana's in trouble. You'll make things worse if we can't help her."

"Penhead," Archie said, but she ran out of the kitchen. They heard her footsteps on the wooden stairs.

"You get it, don't you?" Archie asked Quin. He leaned against the counter and crossed his arms. Quin hesitated. He understood. The mysterious notes and texts and Mariana disappearing all made him nervous. But he knew Pen was right, too. Once their parents knew about their search for the stolen trophy, they probably wouldn't get to leave the house for a month.

"We'll lose the tournament," he mumbled. "And what if Mariana is in danger?"

Archie's face tightened. "I know. That's why I have to tell them."

"I'll be in my studio." Quin left his big brother in the kitchen. When he entered the art studio, the last of the sunlight slid through the windows, tinting his finished model of the golden ball a deep bronze. Quin touched it lightly and wondered if the trophy, and Mariana, were both gone forever.

Pen opened her laptop and slammed her fingertips on the keys. "Traitor," she muttered under her breath. She couldn't remember the last time she'd been so mad at Archie. How could he tell on them knowing they'd miss the tournament and have no chance to find Mariana?

Pen's fingers flew through the security measures and opened SPYder. She found the last message, hit reply, and typed:

We need to talk. I want to help Mariana. Where is she?

She clicked send and started reading another article on the Culper Spy Ring. This article talked about the inner turmoil between some of the group members and how the leader even threatened to quit the ring. Pen gritted her teeth. Archie was part of her inner ring, and Quin, too, but instead of helping Mariana, they were waiting for her parents to get home so Archie could spill everything about their search for the golden ball.

Pen's phone buzzed and she glanced at the new text. The message took her breath away.

Meet at midnight. Soccer field at St. Mary's. Do not call the police.

Pen's door burst open, making Pen yelp and slam her laptop shut.

"Can't you knock?"

Quin shook his head. "Mamá and Dad just got home. I thought you'd want to know."

He held the model of the trophy in his hands. Pen stared at it and sighed. "We were so close," she muttered. She showed him the text on SPYder. His eyes widened.

"Who could this be?"

"Somebody who knows I'm behind SPYder," Pen whispered. "Nobody but Archie knows that, and this isn't Archie." Pen swallowed and almost wished it were her big brother messing around with them.

"Penelope and Quintus Grey Reyes," Mamá shouted up the stairs. "*Ven aquí este momento.*"

Quin groaned. "Time to face the firing squad."

Pen thought of the spies she'd been studying for her project. Not all the spies had been successful. Some had been caught and executed for treachery. "I can't believe he actually did it," she whispered. "Archie ratted us out."

Quin set the model trophy on Pen's desk and they gazed at it solemnly. Pen saluted it and Quin didn't laugh.

"Sorry you won't get to finish the tournament," Pen said, her eyes on the trophy instead of Quin. "I know it meant a lot to you."

Quin blinked and straightened his glasses. "It's just a dumb trophy."

"Right," Pen agreed, thinking of the trophy they'd been

searching for. They looked at each other.

"You know, if we're going to be in trouble anyway, we might as well—" Pen started to say.

"Sneak out," Quin finished. He nodded slowly. "Whoever sent you that message on SPYder must know where Mariana is."

"And the golden ball. We have to go to the meeting tonight."

"If we survive this," her twin said, nodding toward the door and the stairway beyond.

"I'm waiting," Mamá called again.

"Then we're agreed. No matter what happens?"

"It's a pact," Quin said. Then the twins walked downstairs to face their executioners.

Quin sat on his bed, nervously fiddling with his shoelaces and eyeing the clock. Pen crept through the adjoining door at exactly eleven o'clock.

"Ready?"

"Ready if you are," Quin whispered back.

Their parents had been furious at dinner. He could still hear Mamá's heated words in his head. "*No lo creo. I can't believe it. Why wouldn't you tell anyone about Mariana and this trophy?*"

Dad had been calmer but firm when he told the twins they weren't allowed to go anywhere but school and soccer practice until further notice. At least, Quin reflected, they hadn't pulled the twins from the tournament.

Quin stood up and tiptoed to the window. The huge oak tree stretched its dark limbs into the air. The last time Quin had been in a tree, he'd fallen and broken his arm. The idea of climbing out the window made his stomach dance. "I don't know if we should do this."

"Even if it'll save Mariana?" Pen said.

Quin sighed. "That's the only reason to do it."

"We can't get in any more trouble at this point." Pen

started to unlock the window and push it open. He could think of a lot more trouble they could be in, but he didn't mention this.

She paused and both twins listened. No sounds came from their parents' room downstairs, or even from the old house itself. Pen slid the window open and popped the screen out. She placed it on the window seat, then clicked on a flashlight. She cast one look back at Quin. In the dark, her eyes glittered.

"Let's go," he whispered.

Pen put the end of the flashlight in her mouth, climbed out of the window and wrapped her hands and legs around the nearest limb. The tree limb swayed with her weight and one branch scratched the side of the house like fingernails. The sound sent shivers racing down Quin's spine. He clicked on his own flashlight and watched Pen's light bob as she edged her way down the limb to the trunk. The light floated like a ghost lamp in the air for a moment, then flashed on and off twice, Pen's signal for him to climb out.

"You're a goalkeeper," Quin whispered. Darkness yawned below him. "You leap in the air all the time." He rubbed his arm.

"Quin!" Pen's hushed voice rose from somewhere in the dark below him. "Move it."

He ducked through the open window and crawled onto the branch. It swayed under his weight and he wrapped his legs around it. Then he slid the window almost shut behind him, leaving just a crack so they could sneak back in the same way. That wasn't too hard, Quin thought. He started scooting down the limb. Small branches snagged his jeans and brushed his face.

The flashlight grew heavy in his mouth and drool collected around it. He desperately needed to swallow. Keep moving. Nearly there, he thought. The flashlight wobbled and slipped a little. Quin clamped down harder with his teeth. He could see Pen's silhouette camped out a few branches down. What had he been worried about?

Quin picked up his hand and grabbed the trunk. Something skittered across it. Something large with lots of legs. It started climbing his arm.

Spider!

Quin jerked his arm up and shook hard. "Gahhh," he muttered, managing not to scream. He felt proud he'd muffled the sound until he remembered he should have a flashlight in his mouth. "Uh-oh." The flashlight beamed from its spot on the ground into the first-floor window of the Grey Reyes home, his parents' bedroom window.

Quin heard a series of quiet crashes and a short squeal. Then the flashlight below him clicked out, along with Pen's. He couldn't see his sister. In fact, he couldn't see anything. The moon was on the other side of the house. And then light flooded out of his parents' bedroom window and Quin could see everything.

Pen lay frozen on the ground gripping both flashlights to her chest. She rolled once and managed to tuck most of her body beneath the hydrangeas outside the bedroom window. Quin pulled his legs up and balanced on the limb. Below him, his father peered through the window. It felt like light flowed from the bedroom for an eternity. Quin glanced at his arm and noticed a small, harmless cicada perched on it. Stupid bug. He flicked it away and it flew into the night with an insulted clicking sound.

The light below disappeared and Quin released a breath he didn't realize he was holding. Pen rustled out of the bushes. He could make out her shadow crossing the yard. He gritted his teeth and pressed forward. How ironic the last time he'd been in a tree he was trying to escape a thief and now he was heading to meet one.

When Quin's feet finally found solid ground, he hunched over and hurried to the street corner. It was empty. "Pen?" he whispered, slowly turning around. Dark houses and trees loomed around him.

"I can't believe you're our goalkeeper," Pen stepped out of the shadows of the nearest tree. "How do you manage to jump so high without being afraid of the fall?"

"Shove it." They hurried down the sidewalk, stepping around the streetlights when they could. Quin shivered as a breeze rustled the leaves in the trees overhead. They walked down this street every day to catch the bus, but everything looked different at night. The street lights cast strange shadows across the road. Weird shapes loomed ahead of them in the darkness. One turned out to be a trashcan, another a bicycle someone left on the sidewalk.

They hurried down familiar roads while shadows waved across the figures of parked cars, trash cans, and street signs. Once they left the residential streets, traffic increased slightly and they dodged behind trees every time a car rolled by. Quin wondered if they'd ever arrive at this rate, but soon enough, they reached Mission Hill Park. Quin studied the dark interior beyond the arched entryway.

"Let's go around," he whispered.

"That'll take ages," Pen replied. "Are you scared?" She blew out her breath in a husky *whooooooo*. Quin felt something tickle his arm at the same time. He slapped her hand away.

"Stop it. I'm not scared. It's just..." Quin searched for a valid excuse. "You know Mamá doesn't like us in the park after dark."

Pen snorted. He could almost hear his sister's thoughts. If Mamá knew what they were up to, being in the park after dark would be the least of their worries.

"Let's go." Pen grabbed his hand and pulled him forward, squeezing it briefly. At least she was a little scared, too.

They crossed the empty soccer fields and passed the swings. The wind made them creak and move slightly on their chains like ghost children swung on them. Quin shivered. Think about something else, he told himself. But all he could think about was the fact they were meeting a stranger at night and nobody else knew where they were.

"Do you think this is what it feels like to be a spy?" Pen whispered as they reached the park exit and stepped onto the sidewalk. Quin breathed out in relief and felt a little silly.

"If spies meet each other behind their schools the night before the biggest game of their lives, then yes." Now that they were close to their destination, he felt less anxious. They hadn't been caught leaving the house. Nobody had accosted them in the park. Maybe everything was going to be okay.

"I mean like the Culper Spy Ring." Quin could hear a hint of exasperation in her voice. "They used to meet each other in the dead of night like this."

"Do you have to say dead?"

She continued without stopping. "They had two double agents in New York City who would hand off information—" Her voice dropped to a whisper as they approached St. Mary's. "And eventually it got to George Washington. They helped win the war with their spy work. They saved people, just like we're going to save Mariana."

Quin thought about his sister's words, and Mamá's announcement at dinner that the police were searching for Mariana. What if they disappeared tonight, too?

"Did they all make it through the war?" he whispered.

"Who?" They'd reached St. Mary's. Pen was studying the building.

"Your spies."

"Oh." She hesitated. "Almost. One died, though. Agent 355. Nobody even knows her real name. But the others lived and kept their secrets. Nobody knew they were spies until," Pen waved her hand, a shadow in the dark, "about 1930. And then this historian—"

"Hey," Quin interrupted. "Isn't that Sister Doris's office?" He pointed to a window where light streamed through. "What's she doing up so late?"

"Probably praying. Let's go see."

"Pen," he whispered as his sister crouched down and

slipped behind some bushes near the office window. "I don't think—"

But Pen had already popped her head up to the window and peered inside. The light reflected off her face for an instant. Then she gasped and dropped down. She wriggled out of the bushes and scurried to Quin.

"Come on. We have to get to the soccer field now."

"Why? What did you see?"

"The night janitor." She tugged Quin around the side of the school. She leaned over and half ran past the empty classrooms. Quin followed, confused.

"So what? Did he see you?"

Pen didn't answer. She jogged to the end of the building and squatted down. They were at the top of the hill that sloped down to the soccer field. They crouched against the brick wall, still warm with heat from earlier in the day.

Quin squatted down next to his sister. Ahead of them, the field was pitch black, but he didn't care about that right now. He hated it when Pen held him in suspense. "I give up. Why are you worried about the night janitor?"

Pen pointed below them. A flashlight beam swung back and forth across the field, then winked out. "One if by land, two if by sea," Pen whispered.

"Pen, what about the night janitor? Who is he?"

Pen stood up, glanced behind them, and started walking down the stairs to the field. "He's the man in black."

"What do you mean the man in black? What's he doing here?"

Pen didn't answer right away. She had to concentrate on the crumbling stairs leading to the field. She didn't want to risk turning on the flashlight now that she'd seen the man in black in Sister Doris's office. In her chair. Typing on her computer.

"I don't know," Pen finally answered. She strained to see ahead of them. She thought she could make out a dark figure in the center circle.

"But if the man in black is a janitor at St. Mary's, he could have sent the email about the trophy using Mariana's username." He paused. "He's been watching us all along."

Pen didn't answer. The thought was chilling. They reached the soccer field and a shadow loomed ahead of them.

"Is it you?" the shadow called out, the words thick with a foreign accent Pen recognized as Spanish. "Is it SPYder?"

At the words, Pen felt a surge of pride. "Yes," she answered. "Who are you?"

A hand clamped hard on Pen's arm. Pen couldn't help it. She screeched, the noise cutting into the silent night. A rough hand clapped down over her mouth. "Shh. We need to talk."

"Let her go," Quin shouted, his voice high. An extremely long arm shot out and grasped Quin's elbow. "Be quiet." The man's voice was so low Pen could barely hear him. "Or they'll hear us."

"Who?" Pen yelped.

The man tightened his grip on Pen's arm. He started dragging both twins across the field. "I will tell you, but we cannot stay here."

Pen felt like a puppet being jerked by its strings. Adrenaline coursed through her, like it did before she sprinted down the field to score a goal. She kicked out and caught their attacker in the knee.

"Aaaggh!" The man dropped to one knee but he didn't let go. He jerked Pen and Quin so closely together they nearly bashed heads.

"*Silencio* or we will not save Mariana. They will catch us instead."

"Who?" Quin asked.

"Where's Mariana?" Pen added, her voice loud.

"Shh," he said. "Please. Be quiet." He pulled them across the field toward the small set of bleachers.

"We won't," Pen protested. She tried to dig her feet into

the grass but the man was too large and strong. "We'll shout for help."

The man stiffened suddenly. "Did you hear that?" He crouched down near bleachers, pulling the twins down with him. Shouting echoed across the empty field. Their attacker pushed them under the bleachers and did his best to crawl in, too. He was huge, Pen realized. Her fear of him was melting away. He seemed as nervous as them.

"This is the reason I asked you to meet me here," he whispered. "But you must be very quiet."

"Where is it?" A low, gravelly voice floated across the field.

"I need more time. *Por favor*, my daughter—"

"That's Mariana's father," Quin whispered.

"You've had enough time," the low voice said. "I want that trophy or you'll never see your daughter again."

The grip on Pen's arm tightened so much she nearly cried out. "This is all wrong," the man muttered. "He can't have the trophy. I won't let him."

Pen stifled a gasp. "Do you have the trophy?"

"It's safe," the man whispered. "But Mariana is not. That's why you're here."

"Tell us who you are," Pen demanded. "How do we know we can trust you? Maybe you're kidnapping us like you kidnapped Mariana?"

The man's long fingers pinched Pen's shoulder. "I did not take Mariana. I am not like those men. They are—"

A burst of shouting interrupted him. Across the field, Mariana's father screamed in rapid Portuguese, his voice was high-pitched and frantic.

"Tomorrow," the other voice cut through the screaming. "At the tournament. Get the trophy to me or you'll never see her again." They saw a dark shadow cross the field, leaving Mariana's father alone.

"This is all my fault," the man next to Pen whispered. "I did not take the trophy to Daniel. I could not. Luca is my friend. Why did I do it?"

Quin shook her shoulder. "Pen," he said, his voice urgent.

"Do you have the trophy?" She tried to look closer at the man despite the darkness. He wore a baseball cap on his head. Why was he wearing a hat at night?

"Y-yes," he stuttered. "But I must give it to Daniel to save Mariana."

"Pen," her twin said again, insistent. "I know who he is."

The man rose. "There's no time. I must go now and give the trophy to Daniel or we will never find Mariana."

"Wait," Pen said. "We can figure out a way to get Mariana back and not give up the trophy."

The man paused. "How?" he asked.

Pen thought furiously. There had to be a way. Spies did things like this all the time. She thought of the Culper Ring. How had they passed information among their enemy? Encoded messages? Dead drops? Double agents? That was it. She had it.

"Do you still have the phone you contacted SPYder with?"

Yes," the man said.

"I'll contact you and tell you what to do. I think there's a way we can find Mariana and keep the trophy away from them."

Suddenly, a phone rang right next to them. The man cursed and fumbled in his jacket pocket for it.

"Sal?" Mariana's father called out from midfield. "Are you here?"

"Go," the man whispered. "I will wait for your text, but now I have to tell Daniel why I didn't bring him the trophy tonight. He won't be happy."

"Sal?" Quin said. "That's your name?"

The man waved them off. "Go now. Before Daniel sees you, and stay away from the school. They are always watching. They might be watching us now."

He stood up and jogged toward Mariana's father. "Daniel," he said. "Sorry I am late. Did you meet already?"

Mariana's father let loose what Pen thought to be a string of curse words in Portuguese.

The twins crept out the other side of the bleachers and hurried down the road, away from St. Mary's.

This could be a trap," Pen whispered, her mind trying to sort out the strange conversation. "We don't know who he is or if we can trust him."

"I know who he is." Quin's voice trembled with excitement. "That's what I kept trying to tell you."

Pen stopped walking. "You do?" She glanced around and didn't see anyone, but it was so dark that didn't mean much.

"Mariana's father called him Sal. You saw how big he was. He's friends with Luca. Pen, that could only be one person."

Pen shook her head. She was missing something huge and Quin wasn't. She was supposed to be the spy. She sighed. "Okay, who do you think it is?"

"Salvatore Cienfuegos."

"The Spanish goalkeeper? But why—oh. I get it. He was in Spain with Luca. He could have stolen the trophy and brought it here."

"Exactly," Quin said, his voice despondent. "But why would he do that to Luca?"

A man stepped out into the street in front of them. "It's a little late to be at school, isn't it?"

Pen gasped and turned to run, but the man in black was too fast. He grabbed both twins and held them with an iron grip. "And defacing school property at that. I think Sister Doris needs to know about this." He began dragging them back to St. Mary's.

"Defacing school property? We didn't do anything," Pen shouted. "Let us go."

"Then what are you doing out here?" the man asked them. The twins said nothing.

"I see," the man said. "Then I caught you red-handed. This is the end of the tournament for you both." He pulled them up the stairs and into the school. The light from Sister Doris's office still shone down the hall. The man gave the twins a cruel smile. "And if you know what's good for you, you'll stay out of Daniel da Silva's way or you'll end up like your friend, Mariana. And we don't want that, do we?"

He shoved them into two office chairs and pulled a phone from his pocket. The person on the other end must have picked up because the man's face smoothed into a smile.

"Hello, Sister. So sorry to call this late. I've just caught two students trespassing and destroying school property. I think you'd better come down."

Pen shifted in her seat and eyed the door. The man narrowed his eyes and shook his head slowly. "Their names? Penelope and Quintus Grey Reyes."

When he hung up, his eyes grew cold. "Now, tell me everything you know about the Ballon d'Or."

At first they'd kept their mouths shut, but after two minutes of silence, the man in black's sun wrinkled face, one Pen hadn't seen up close until now, turned dark.

"Don't forget I know many things about you both. Where you live, who your friends are, your class schedules, your family." He shoved an oversized nose too close to Pen's face. "You do not want to cross me, children."

Pen wrinkled her nose at the man's breath. He wasn't American, but she couldn't identify his accent. It was smooth and nondescript, and certainly not Portuguese, like Mariana, or the thick Spanish of Salvatore Cienfuegos, if Quin was right about his guess.

A thousand thoughts thundered through Pen's head and raced away as she tried to grasp them. She was only sure of one thing. This man meant what he said. He would harm them. Maybe not tonight with Sister Doris on her way, but sometime, and they wouldn't know when.

"We don't know anything about the stolen trophy," Quin said. "Only that it's missing, like Mariana," he said accusingly.

"But you've been looking for it." The man in black stood too close to them. Pen could see the individual black hairs on his jaw. "You and Mariana and your big brother, too."

"You've been spying on us," Pen spat. "Ever since school started. You're not a janitor."

The man in black shrugged. "I have kept Mariana close. That meant I needed a way inside your school."

"But you tried to take her after our soccer scrimmage. You were at her apartment. You climbed on the roof. I followed you but you disappeared."

The man grinned and snapped his fingers. "Yes. Poof. Like magic."

Quin's voice chimed in, a little shaky. "You tried to run me over."

Pen looked at her brother, stunned. She hadn't put this chain of events together, but she could see by the man in black's face Quin was right.

"Not run over, merely scare off," the man shrugged, then frowned. "It didn't work. You two do not scare easily." He nodded at them almost admiringly. "But now you must." Once again he leaned so close Pen could smell his rank breath.

"Do not come to the fields tomorrow. Stay home like good children and this will all be over. If you do not—" he paused and snapped his fingers again. "Poof."

The office door opened and Sister Doris puffed in, out of breath, dressed in jeans and a T-shirt and only a scarf wrapped around her head with rumpled grey curls sticking out from beneath it.

"Good heavens. What is this all about, Mr. Jackson?" She directed her steely eyes on Pen and Quin. "What in heaven's name are you two doing here at this time of night, with your last game of the tournament tomorrow morning, no less?"

Was it Pen's imagination, or did Sister Doris sound more distraught over the game than them being at school?

"We were searching for Mariana." Quin slumped in his

chair and didn't meet Sister Doris's eyes. "We thought maybe she'd come back here."

Pen saw the hard look in Sister Doris's eyes soften slightly. "But of course she's not here. The police still haven't found her. And they searched the school earlier. I was here myself when they did."

"Oh," Pen said, deflated.

Sister Doris shook her head. "I admire your concern for your friend, though your timing is misguided, but why deface those lockers? I saw the graffiti all over them when I came in the door."

"We didn't do that," Pen burst out. She glared at the man in black. "He's lying. And he's not the janitor. He's the man in black. He knows where Mariana is. Ask him."

"Penelope Grey Reyes," Sister Doris said, the sternness back in her voice. "Get yourself under control."

"She's been like that since I caught them," the man in black said smoothly. "Raving about spies and trophies and," he paused and chuckled, "me. And here I thought kids just ignored the janitor."

"I'm not raving," Pen shouted.

"*Calmaté*," Quin whispered. She knew he was right, but she felt the anger bubbling within her.

"He's lying," she said again.

"I'm going to the lockers to see what can be done about the graffiti," the man in black said. "When their parents get here, you can join me."

"Thank you, Mr. Jackson," Sister Doris said. "Adam and Maria should be here any moment."

The man in black pulled open the office door and stepped through. Sister Doris kept her gaze on the twins. She crossed her arms and tapped one foot on the floor. "I want an explanation."

Behind her, the man in black gave Pen and Quin a cold glare and silently snapped his fingers. "Poof," he mouthed, then shut the door behind him.

19

When Quin woke up the next morning, he hoped with all his might last night had been a dream. Maybe Mariana wasn't still missing. Maybe he'd only dreamed he and Pen had snuck out to St. Mary's and gotten caught by the school janitor, who was actually the man in black. Maybe his parents hadn't come to St. Mary's for them at midnight, bewildered. And when they trooped down the hall to see the lockers scrawled in permanent marker with words Quin had never even thought of using, they couldn't find the janitor anywhere.

Sister Doris insisted they all go home and talk about the incident after the soccer game the next morning. She'd looked at them regretfully.

"Both of you will not play in the game. However, I'd like you to attend to cheer on your teammates, as I expect the Saints will need all the help they can get now."

With that she dismissed them all and Mamá and Dad lectured them on the way home about not sneaking out, even if they were searching for Mariana. Fortunately, they believed Quin's claims they hadn't touched the lockers or even been inside the school. Pen remained uncharacteristically silent, and he couldn't understand why until they'd both been sent to their rooms and she crept through the bathroom to sit on his bed.

"I sent the next message to Salvatore Cienfuegos." She hesitated, then added, "I told him my plan."

"What is it?" Quin asked warily. He drew the covers up to his chin and resisted the urge to kick Pen off his bed. He couldn't believe they would miss the game in the morning. A glance at the bedside clock told him it was nearly 2:00 a.m. Technically, it was already morning.

Pen leaned over and whispered her idea, which made him sit up straight. "Do you think it will work?"

"It has to, or we may never see Mariana again."

When Pen and Quin arrived at the Saints' game the next morning dressed only in their blue warm-ups instead of uniforms, Coach Sikes crossed his arms, puffed out his cheeks and said, "I hear you have a story for us."

The frown on his face made Pen think he'd already heard the details. The Saints gathered around while the twins took turns telling the story of the night before. At least the one they'd told their parents and Sister Doris about searching for Mariana. Of course, they didn't say the school janitor was the man in black, but they admitted being on school property after hours. When Pen finished the story with their suspension from the game, their teammates all stared in silence.

"Is that story for real?" Michael asked.

"Of course it is," Pen snapped. "Why would we make it up?"

"And you didn't think to call me?" Michael asked. "I could've helped."

"Yeah, that's right," echoed around the circle of Saints.

"Okay, that's enough," Coach Sikes said. His face mirrored the gray clouds overhead. "Mariana's disappearance is a police matter. I've been assured they're looking for her throughout the city. If everyone had snuck out," he gave Pen and Quin a stern look, "then I wouldn't have anyone left to put on the field against the Santos. As it is, we're down three players today."

Pen gazed across the field where the Santos were warming up. Their crisp white and black uniforms seemed even brighter against the gray sky. An assistant coach shouted at the team. She turned back to her own team-mates, the ones who wished they'd been with Pen and Quin last night to search for Mariana. What had she been afraid of when Mariana walked onto the soccer field the first time?

Having Mariana on the team made the Saints stronger, and Pen had to admit, she liked the girl, even if it meant she didn't get to play as much. And now she might not see Mariana again, unless she could put her plan in motion.

"I guess I'll have to score all the goals," Michael quipped. Pen leveled him with a cool gaze. "Just one goal would be good today."

"Okay," Coach Sikes said. "Blalock will play up front with Gonzalez."

Pen winced and glanced at the small fifth-grade forward. Gabriel had just made the team this year.

"Me?" he whispered, his mouth wide open.

Coach Sikes continued to roll off the starting lineup. When he finished with the defense, he paused and sighed. "You're in goal, Leary. You'll have to be big for us today."

Dennis looked petrified. Every freckle on his face stood out against his pale skin. The Saints circled up and put their hands in the center. "You too," Coach Sikes told the twins. "You're still part of this team."

"Go Saints," they cheered. Pen tried to shout with her usual enthusiasm, but part of her ached as she watched Michael and Gabriel trot onto the field. Quin grabbed Dennis Leary and put one hand on each shoulder.

"Listen," Quin said. "You can do this."

Dennis nodded numbly and stared at the Brazilians taking the field. "They're so big," he whispered. "And fast."

"Doesn't matter," Quin said. "You have the best defense in the world in front of you. All you have to do is trust them. Being able to trust your teammates, that's what makes a great keeper." Quin's voice faltered. Pen watched her brother carefully. Since finding out Salvatore Cienfuegos was somehow involved in stealing the trophy, Quin had hardly said a word to anyone.

"You think so?" Dennis asked. His face held a little more color and he gazed at Quin with big blue eyes. "I'll think about Salvatore Cienfuegos, like you always do."

Quin's face flushed deep red. "No," he said. "Just think about the Saints and how cool it is to be playing with them in the Friendship Cup. That's all you need."

"It is cool." Dennis turned to the field and started walking toward the Saints' goal.

Quin grinned. "Go get them, Leary," he shouted. Pen stepped up beside him. "I think that kid's going to be okay, but I don't want to watch this game."

"Good thing we don't have to. Time to put our last spy mission into play."

The referee blew the whistle and the Santos kicked off. They immediately attacked, driving right through the midfield, but a powerful blast from Lyla sent the ball soaring back up the field toward Michael. The Saints' parents and fans on the sidelines erupted in cheers as Michael deftly trapped the ball out of the air with his left foot and sprinted downfield. Pen held her breath while Michael took a hard shot the Santos goalkeeper deflected just wide of the goal.

"You know, if Michael scores all the goals today, he'll be impossible," she told Quin.

"Look," Quin whispered and gestured to their parents. Dad and Mamá were watching the game intently. He pointed to the backpack he wore on his back. "We have to go now, while everyone's distracted."

The twins backed slowly away from the sidelines until they were behind the crowd. Then they sprinted away from the field.

"Do you see him?" Quin asked as they ducked through the crowds of players and parents milling around the fields. Pen scanned the crowd for a tall figure. "No." She hoped Cienfuegos hadn't backed out of the plan. Her heart started to pound. This was it. A planned dead drop, just like the Culper Spy Ring. "Let's get to that table."

"Uh-oh," Quin said. "Archie and Luca are here."

Pen swung around and saw their older brother and Luca drifting through the crowd. The wind whipped Archie's hair around crazily. Luca wore a Real Madrid cap to hide his face.

A roar erupted from the direction of the Saints versus Santos game, and Archie and Luca turned toward it.

"Quick, before they see us." Pen pulled the backpack off Quin's back and shoved it in his hands. He unzipped the pack and carefully pulled his model of the golden ball free. They hurried to the check-in tent, which had been transformed. Instead of paper and pens, it held gleaming trophies for first, second, and third place, plus individual medals and trophies for most valuable player, the most goals scored, and the best goalkeeper.

Sitting in the middle of the Friendship Cup trophies, the Ballon d'Or gleamed even in the low light of a cloudy morning. "It's beautiful," Pen whispered. She felt relieved Cienfuegos had come through with his end of the deal. She carefully looked around but with the large crowd milling about the tent, even Cienfuegos's tall figure wasn't easy to spot. She finally saw him standing near the edge of the crowd with the Red Sox cap pulled over his face and his jacket zipped up to his chin.

Quin placed the model trophy on the table and put the real golden ball in his backpack. As he zipped it shut, a voice piped behind them. "Where are you taking the trophy?"

A small girl eyed them suspiciously. She scratched her nose and pointed to Quin's bag. "I saw you put that trophy in your bag," she said, louder than Pen would have liked.

"We're taking it to get cleaned," Quin said. "You know, before the tournament is over."

The girl scowled. "It looked clean to me."

"Oh, never mind," Pen said. She glanced back at the table. The fake trophy was gone. "Quin," she gasped and pointed to a tall figure hurrying through the crowd. "Cienfuegos has it. Let's go."

"Go where?" Quin acted like she'd just asked him to play for the Santos. "I thought we were supposed to give the real trophy to the police. Isn't that the plan you worked out with Cienfuegos last night?"

Pen watched the disappearing goalkeeper. "That's what I told him." She grabbed the backpack from Quin's hands. "Here," she said, shoving it at the girl. "Do you see the man over there in the Real Madrid hat?"

The girl nodded.

"That's Luca. This is his trophy. Take it to him. Tell him you found it."

The girl's eyes grew wide. "Really?"

"Pen, I don't think this—" Quin started to say.

"Really." She turned the girl around and pushed her in Luca's direction. Luca looked up and spotted the twins. "Oh no, he saw us."

"Isn't that Luca da Silva?" Quin called out. He pointed straight to Luca. A few people in the crowd followed his gesture. One by one, players recognized the best footballer in the world.

"Luca!" they shouted and pressed forward, calling out for autographs and pictures. Luca shook his head at the twins, frustration playing across his face.

"Sorry," Quin mouthed to Luca.

"Brilliant diversion tactic," Pen said. "Let's go find Mariana."

She sprinted away from the tent with Quin by her side, both of them chasing Salvatore Cienfuegos.

Cienfuegos hurried across the park, away from the soccer fields. Quin grabbed his sister's hand and forced her to slow down. She shot him an annoyed look, but he put a finger to his lips and pointed. Ahead of them, Cienfuegos had slowed to a walk. He looked around and the twins dodged behind a large tree.

"Why didn't you tell me you planned to follow him?" Quin gritted his teeth. Why couldn't Pen ever share her thoughts with him?

"Why didn't you guess?" Pen hissed.

True. He should have anticipated this.

"This way we can be sure Cienfuegos exchanges the trophy for Mariana and she's safe," Pen said.

"Except the trophy's not real. It won't take the man in black long to figure that out."

Pen pulled her phone out of her pocket. Fortunately, her parents hadn't taken it away last night. "I'll call the police as soon as we know where they're keeping Mariana."

Quin peered out from behind the tree. "He's on the move."

Cautiously, they followed Cienfuegos across the green lawn and walking trail toward the river bank, where the park ended at the Charles River.

"Why is he going to the river?" Pen muttered.

A hand landed on Quin's shoulder. Luca, Quin thought. He turned, already thinking of how to explain himself to the footballer. But it wasn't Luca's face that greeted him.

"Hello Quin," the man in black said. He wore a black Santos hat and his eyes underneath weren't friendly. His hand slid down to grip Quin's elbow.

"You're supposed to be meeting Cienfuegos," Pen gasped.

The man in black nodded. "Yes, they're waiting for us now." He reached out to grab Pen but she dodged away. "I'm calling the police." She waved the phone in the air. The man's eyes narrowed. "Go ahead. I'll drag your brother to the river and drown him before they arrive."

Quin gulped. "Get help," he told Pen.

She shook her head. "I'm not leaving."

"Good," the man in black said. "We'll all go get the trophy together. Hand me that phone, Penelope. And don't try to send any texts."

Pen froze and looked from Quin to the man in black. Her mouth hardened. Quin knew that look. "Pen," he cautioned, but his sister cocked her arm and threw the phone away. It sailed through the air and clattered onto the gravel walking trail. Pen winced, probably thinking of the scratches the phone had endured.

The man in black's hand shot out and grabbed Pen's wrist. "Very stupid, but it doesn't matter." He pulled both twins with him, his hands like iron shackles. Quin felt the pressure on his arm and hoped the bone wouldn't break again. Maybe, he told himself, Pen had already contacted the police. He tried to catch her eye across the man in black's chest. Pen dragged her feet and stared behind her.

"Walk," the man in black ordered.

Pen straightened up and turned to Quin, her eyes wide. "Look," she mouthed. Quin frowned and tried to glance over his shoulder but the man gripped him tighter.

"Where's Mariana?" he asked.

The man in black shrugged. "You'll see."

"*Ajude me*," a voice shouted from beyond the river bank. "Help me!"

"That's Mariana," Pen shouted. She twisted free of the man in black and sprinted for the river.

"Hey," the man shouted, and dragged Quin roughly down the steep bank to the water's edge. Quin stumbled and fell as the grass softened into sticky, black mud.

Cienfuegos and Daniel da Silva stood on the river bank. They stared at the twins with open mouths.

"What are they doing here?" Mariana's father said, his fury barely contained. If Quin didn't know better, he would have thought Mariana's father was concerned for them. Cienfuegos held Quin's trophy to his chest. Quin felt a brief flash of pride. From here, the trophy looked real.

A low rumble of thunder rolled across the sky and

raindrops splattered the river's surface.

"Mariana," Pen called out. She pointed to a red canoe slowly drifting down the river. One man paddled the canoe, dressed in black, nearly a mirror image of the man on shore. Twins, Quin thought. That's why we thought we saw the man in black everywhere. There were two of them. In the front of the canoe, Mariana waved frantically. She still wore her blue Saints jersey.

"Mariana," Daniel da Silva gasped. He turned to Cienfuegos. "Give me the trophy."

Cienfuegos shook his head. "No. Not until Mariana is safe."

If Mariana's father got the trophy, he'd realize it wasn't real before Mariana was on shore. Quin didn't think about it. He dashed past the man in black and Daniel da Silva and tugged the trophy out of Cienfuegos' hands. He scrambled into the thick mud at the water's edge, feeling the sludge cover his shoes.

"What are you doing?" Daniel da Silva shouted.

The man in black reacted quickly, but he didn't go after Quin. He picked Pen up and lifted her over the water. Quin gasped and held the trophy even tighter while he watched Pen kick the air.

"Give it to da Silva," the man in black ordered.

"No," Pen shrieked. "Quin, don't. I can swim."

Quin held the trophy out over the muddy water with both hands. "Let her go," he said, his voice shaking. "You don't get it until Pen and Mariana are both safe."

"Sal, get him," Mariana's father ordered.

Cienfuegos shook his head. "No," he said. "I am finished with this." He looked at Quin. *Lo siento.* His voice grew raspy and he blinked several times. "All of this—it was a mistake and I am sorry." Cienfuegos backed away from the group and climbed the river bank.

"Where are you going?" Mariana's father shouted, his voice a screech. "Get back here."

"Let him go," the man in black said. "We don't need him

anymore."

Quin felt his heart sink like he'd already dropped the trophy into the water. Cienfuegos disappeared beyond the river bank. He'd abandoned them.

"Quin, watch out," Pen shouted.

Quin looked back in time to see the canoe driving straight toward him. He jerked sideways to get out of the way, but the muddy river bottom held his feet firmly in place. Quin dove into the water, trophy and all, as the canoe shot past him and into the bank.

He came up spluttering for air and heard Pen shouting. He blinked water out of his eyes and saw Mariana leap to shore. Daniel da Silva rushed to her. The man in black deposited Pen into the canoe. She tried to jump out but the other man dragged her back.

"Give me the trophy." The man in black's voice was loud and harsh. He whipped one strong arm around Pen's neck and shoulders.

"Don't give it to him." She wiggled in the man's arms and he shouted at her to stop.

"Give it to him, Quin," Daniel da Silva yelled from the river bank. Quin gasped for breath and tried to think. He held the trophy out over the water, his arm shaking from the effort.

Water ran off the gold paint and dripped into the river. Thunder cracked overhead and rain pelted down. Quin squinted through the sheet of water at the man in black.

"You want the trophy?" He pulled the heavy model back. "Catch."

He threw the golden ball as high and as far from the canoe as he could. The man in black's mouth dropped open.

"No," he cried. He dove out of the canoe, arms outstretched like a goalkeeper trying to save the winning goal. But the man in black wasn't a goalkeeper. The model trophy plunked into the muddy, brown water and disappeared. The man in black hit the water in a grand bellyflop. Quin would have laughed if things weren't so serious.

"Pen, jump!"

Pen vaulted from the canoe and splashed into the river. The other man shouted, but he was trying to keep the canoe from tipping. The twins slogged through the water to the riverbank. When they reached solid ground, they turned back to the river. The man in black dove into the water, came up empty-handed, and dove again.

The other man shouted at him from the canoe in a language Quin didn't understand. He sat down and began paddling the canoe away from the man in black.

"Pen, Quin," Mariana shouted. She ran to them and hugged them. Daniel da Silva put a hand on Quin's shoulder, but his touch was soft this time, and his voice even softer.

"Quintus," he said. "You do not know what you have done. These men—" his voice broke.

"I know. They're the men who forced you to throw those games, who threatened you and your family, who made you steal Luca's trophy."

"Papai, is that true?" Mariana asked. "You stole Luca's trophy?"

Daniel da Silva's shoulders slumped. "*Sim*, it's true. Without the trophy, we will never be safe."

"We need the police," Quin said.

"Already taken care of." Pen pointed up the riverbank.

"Put your hands up," a loud voice shouted. Policemen stood at the top. Archie, Luca, Ms. Morgan, and Eileen Esposito stood with them. Several more officers slid down the muddy bank to the river.

The man in black floundered in the water and shouted at his twin. The man in the canoe paddled harder down river.

"We'll take it from here," an officer said. He gestured for Pen and Quin to climb up the bank. Then he reached out and took Daniel da Silva's arm. "You're under arrest for international theft."

"No," Mariana cried out. "They made him steal the trophy."

Daniel da Silva drew her into a hug. "I'm sorry, Mariana. I had to do it to keep you safe. Go with your friends," he said, nodding at Pen and Quin.

Tears mingled with raindrops on Mariana's face. Quin gently took her arm and together the three climbed to the top of the bank. A dizzying array of police greeted them, their squad cars flashing. Salvatore Cienfuegos stood next to one, his head down. Quin swallowed the desire to call out to the Spanish goalkeeper.

Ms. Morgan and Eileen Esposito stood with another policeman.

"What are they doing here?" Quin asked.

Pen grinned. "It was Eileen. I saw her in the park when the man in black captured us. I knew Eileen Esposito was following us around." Her smiled dampened a little. "I think she got Ms. Morgan and called the police. That means we owe her."

Archie hurried over with Luca, who held Quin's backpack in his arms. He unzipped it and pulled out the real Ballon d'Or. A shaft of sunlight pushed through the clouds and hit the trophy, causing it to gleam brighter.

His eyes drifted to where the police now held the man in black, Daniel da Silva, and Salvatore Cienfuegos with their hands in handcuffs. The rest of the police officers had fanned out down the riverbank to track the man in the canoe. Luca sighed and rubbed one hand across his eyes. "All of this for one trophy. I wish I'd never won it."

"But you didn't do anything wrong," Pen protested.

Luca's green eyes flicked to her and back to the trophy. "No, but it doesn't make it hurt less." He paused and shook his head. "And if I'd known Daniel was in trouble, that these men told him to get the trophy or they would hurt my family—" He stopped talking and held the trophy out to Quin. Quin took it, noticing the trophy was much heavier than his model. Up close, he realized his model would never have passed for the real trophy. Fortunately, it didn't have to.

"This is yours." He pushed the trophy toward Luca.

Luca gave a sober smile. "You found it. You keep it." He threw one arm around Mariana and together they walked toward Daniel da Silva.

"Wow," Quin breathed, staring at the trophy in his hands. He hefted it into the air.

Pen beamed at him. "You know, I think the Ballon d'Or does look better in a goalkeeper's hands."

"Excuse me," a police officer interrupted. "We need to take that as evidence."

He held out his arms. Quin sighed and placed the trophy into them. "Easy come, easy go."

"What I don't understand is where the real trophy came from?" Archie said, putting one hand on each twin's shoulder. "A girl walked up to Luca and handed it to him."

"I used SPYder to set up a dead drop with Cienfuegos once we learned he had the trophy," Pen said.

Archie's eyebrows shot up. "What? When did you learn that?"

"Last night on a reconnaissance trip to St. Mary's." Archie opened his mouth to say something else, but Pen spoke before he could. "Oh, that reminds me." She led her brothers to a policeman standing next to Cienfuegos. Luca stood next to his best friend, looking as if he'd lost the World Cup. Maybe even worse.

"Salvatore Cienfuegos didn't want Mariana's dad to give the trophy to these men," Pen said. She glared at the man in black, who looked bedraggled in his wet clothes. "He's been trying to help us get it back to Luca."

Cienfuegos hung his head. "Gracias," he whispered. "But I should not have let it be stolen in the first place." He raised his head and met Luca's eyes. "It was my job to make sure you were out of your apartment the night your trophy was stolen."

"Why, Sal?" Luca whispered.

"This was my third time to be nominated for the Ballon d'Or. I thought this time might be different." He sighed. "But do you think a goalkeeper will ever win? No," he answered his own question.

"Always it is a striker. The new young player who scores so many goals. Do they ever stop to think how many goals I save? But that is not what's important in soccer. It is only the balls that go in the net that matter."

Quin found himself nodding. He stopped. He couldn't forget what Cienfuegos had done, even if he was sorry in the end.

"So you let them steal the trophy because you think you should have won," Quin said quietly.

Cienfuegos sighed. "I wanted the world to know the game is not about one man who scores all the goals. But after they stole the trophy, I realized I'd made a big mistake. I found the man who'd stolen the trophy for Daniel in Spain, but he'd already shipped it to Boston. I had to get it back. When I got here, I picked up the trophy and kept it instead of taking it to Daniel like we agreed. I knew it might put the da Silvas in danger, so I tried to help Mariana." He glanced at Pen and Quin. "And you two, when I realized you were looking for the trophy."

"That was you in the donut shop," Quin said.

"And you put the note in Quin's soccer ball, and you saved him from being hit by the car," Pen added.

Cienfuegos nodded. "Those men have been following Mariana since she arrived. They wanted to make sure Daniel agreed to give them the trophy by intimidating his family."

Luca put a hand on Cienfuegos' shoulder. "I would have given you the trophy if you had asked."

The policeman grabbed Cienfuegos' handcuffed arms. "Time to go. We'll sort all of this out at the station."

"Wait," Quin called out.

Cienfuegos turned to Quin and gave him a sad smile. "Sí, goalkeeper?"

"How did you know we were looking for the golden ball in the first place?"

Cienfuegos' face turned as red as his hair. He fumbled with something in his back pocket, his hands still cuffed together. "Here." He shoved something at Quin. "Sorry."

"My phone." Quin took his phone, noticing a few small scratches across the side.

Cienfuegos shrugged. "It fell from your pocket when I pulled you away from the car. I decided to keep it. I thought it might be good to have a way to reach you since you were Mariana's friends and she was in danger. Then I found your text from SPYder and decided to use it."

"How did you know I was behind SPYder?" Pen demanded.

Eileen Esposito pushed past the policeman and stepped into the group. "Seriously, Pen? Everyone knew."

Pen shot Eileen a furious look and opened her mouth. Then closed it. "Oh," she muttered instead. Eileen held out Pen's phone. Pen took it and rubbed at a scratch on the case. "Thanks. For everything."

Quin smothered a smile, though not before his twin caught the corners of his mouth tipping up and glared at him. His sister would find owing Eileen Esposito difficult.

One of the policemen motioned to Pen, Quin, Luca, and Archie. "I need all of you to come down and make statements. You too, ma'am," he told Ms. Morgan. "And these minors need their parents with them."

"Hey, where are Mamá and Dad?" Quin asked.

Archie shook his head. "I never made it to your game. When that girl handed us the trophy, we started to look for you."

"Your parents were still at the game when Eileen got me," Ms. Morgan said. The rain had caused her curls to fall around her face and now her hair was beginning to frizz out. "I didn't know if Eileen was telling the truth. I thought it best to see what was happening before I alarmed anyone."

Eileen looked offended, but she didn't protest.

"The game!" Quin shouted. "Who won?"

"Looks like we're about to find out." Pen nodded toward a group of people hurrying across the park toward them. They recognized Mamá and Dad at the front, with Mariana's mother right behind them.

"We may not play soccer for the rest of the year," Quin sighed.

They watched Mariana's mother rush to her husband and hug him before the police put him in the squad car. Mariana turned away and fled into her mother's arms. Luca hugged them both.

"Do you think Mariana's father will go to jail?" Quin asked.

His twin answered. "I don't know. But we found the trophy and Mariana's safe." Her voice grew stronger. "We solved the case, and if we don't get to play again this year, it's okay."

20

"How does this crepe paper look over the door? Should we add some more orange and yellow and twist it together?"

Eileen held up the streamers of yellow, red, and orange paper. Pen sat on the bleachers, watching her classmates transform the gym into a harvest themed utopia complete with pumpkins, hay bales, and plenty of crepe paper.

"Penelope?" Eileen called out. "I need your help."

She sighed. Helping her class get ready for the Fall Fest was Ms. Morgan's suggestion. When the police questioned Pen and Quin's involvement in the recovery of the stolen trophy, Pen had been forced to admit she was behind SPYder. The first thing her parents demanded she do was apologize to Sister Doris for turning St. Mary's upside down. In the parent meeting, Pen wondered if Sister Doris would suspend her, or at least give her a semester's worth of afternoon detentions. That's when Ms. Morgan stepped in.

"I could use a personal assistant," she said. "Someone to straighten up the classroom and help with odd projects. I think Pen would be perfect. Of course, it will mean some after school time."

Sister Doris weighed the suggestion with pursed lips, finally agreeing if Pen still wrote a formal apology to the entire school for her actions, which of course, her parents guaranteed she would do.

Once the school knew, some unexpected things happened. First, kids began admitting to which texts they'd sent and asked her for further advice. Pen didn't know what to think when Eileen admitted she'd sent texts about her family being in trouble because her mother and father were splitting up.

When Ms. Morgan suggested Pen and Eileen work together on the Fall Fest decorations, Eileen had been delighted. She immediately began to draw a design of the gym and where the refreshments, photo booth, and hay bale maze would be located. Ms. Morgan had given Pen a pained smile and whispered, "Sometimes even the best spies have to learn to work with people they don't like. Give Eileen a chance."

So Pen hung crepe paper across the entry way, twisting it to Eileen's satisfaction. She had to admit, the gym did look festive. "It looks great. You have an eye for this."

Eileen darted a quick glance at her. Pen realized the girl probably thought she was teasing. "Honest."

Eileen's smile lit up her face. She put the leftover crepe paper in a box. "You know, SPYder helped me. Your last text about trusting the people around me made me realize I didn't trust anyone, and I needed to start. That's kind of why I've been following you. I wanted to see if it was you sending those texts."

Eileen's frankness caught Pen by surprise. "I'm glad you did follow me, otherwise, I might not be here." Pen returned the smile.

"Maybe we can curl your hair for the dance," Eileen suggested as they gazed at the harvest wonderland.

"Don't push it." Pen laughed to let Eileen know she wasn't mad. "We don't get to dance anyway. We'll be at the refreshment table all night."

At least this took away the sting that Michael had asked Mariana to the dance and not her. She wondered why Eileen had agreed to man the refreshment table with her.

"Well," Eileen said in reply, twisting one of her perfect curls, "that doesn't mean they can't look."

Pen burst out laughing and Eileen joined in. Maybe, Pen thought, just maybe Ms. Morgan was right.

Quin stared at his phone and tried to stay calm. He sat in his art studio, the fall sunlight dappling the windows through the red and orange trees outside. He'd pulled up Anna's number after sneaking the phone out of Mamá's study. Mamá had confiscated the twins' phones as part of being grounded for the next month. No texts, phone calls, or time spent with friends outside of school, with two exceptions: soccer and the Fall Fest dance. Since Pen had to work the dance, they'd decided to let Quin go too, as long as he volunteered to help.

Quin's finger shook as he touched the call button and held the phone to his ear. Soon Anna's voice came through the other line. She didn't even bother to say hello.

"I thought you were grounded like Pen." Anna's voice was flat.

Quin sucked in a deep breath. He'd had an apology rehearsed in his head, but now all the words ran away like spilled paint.

"I'm sorry we didn't tell you about the golden ball. We shouldn't," he paused, "I mean, I shouldn't have treated you like that, Anna. But things were getting dangerous and I didn't want you to get hurt."

Quin waited. Nothing.

"And so, I'm really sorry," he offered again. "I hope we can still finish the project." He glanced at the painting he'd been working on, a scene of Paul Revere's ride with two lights shining in the tower. "I'm nearly done with my painting," he added. "It'll be perfect with your poem."

Anna had told him she was rewriting Longfellow's famous poem of the ride of Paul Revere and putting a modern spin on it.

"Is that all?" Anna finally said. Her tone wasn't cold, but it wasn't the warmth Quin had felt when they met at D'lite Donuts.

"Uh..." Quin stammered, not sure what else to say.

Anna sighed. "See you in class, Quin."

"Wait—" he shouted. Nothing. Surely Anna had hung up.

"Yes?"

Quin breathed a sigh of relief, but realized he still had no idea what to say. His eyes fell on the unfinished painting of Salvatore Cienfuegos. The police had released the Spanish goalkeeper when Luca decided not to press charges against his friend or his uncle. Instead, Luca returned to Spain with the Ballon d'Or.

Once, Quin reflected, he'd thought he'd never be able to fill shoes as big as Cienfuegos, but the goalkeeper had turned out to be human. A human who could fly through the air to make amazing saves, but still a human. Time to take a chance, Quin thought.

"I can't take you to the dance anymore because I'm grounded. Technically, I'll be there but I have to run the photo booth. Would you want to help me? We'll just be taking pictures all night."

When Anna answered, Quin could hear her smile through the phone. "Of course I'll help. Who cares if we dance or take pictures?" When Quin hung up, he wandered into the living room and flipped on the TV. He found the game he was looking for. The Real Madrid midfielder slid a pass through two defenders and Luca rushed forward. He touched the ball once, twice, and blasted it into the back of the net. The crowd went crazy.

Quin smiled, glad his new friend was back at the sport he loved and the golden ball was back where it belonged too. He watched as the game resumed and Luca fired off another shot. This time the keeper made a spectacular dive and pushed the ball just wide of the goal posts. Quin's eyes widened and he noted the player's name. He was new. A rookie, but that goalkeeper just might be worth watching.

Kind of like Dennis Leary, who'd proven a suitable backup by holding the Santos to only one goal when the Saints tied them in the Friendship Cup. That tie wasn't enough to get the Saints to the final game, though, and the Santos won the tournament and took the Friendship Cup trophy back to Brazil. Quin hadn't minded so much.

Archie came downstairs dressed in old jeans and a T-shirt that said, "I Know HTML." Underneath that it read, "How to Meet Ladies." Pen had actually rolled on the floor laughing when Archie first brought the shirt home.

"More like how to meet losers," she told Archie. It hadn't deterred him from wearing the shirt.

They watched Luca perform a series of step-overs, then burst past a defender with blazing speed. "That kid's got talent." Archie grinned and winked. Quin knew he and Luca had kept in touch since Luca returned to Spain. Quin felt a little jealous, but he'd decided having an older brother who was friends with the best soccer player in the world was better than not knowing Luca at all.

"Do you regret it?" Archie asked.

"What?" Quin looked away from the TV. His older brother's usually laughing eyes were serious.

"Helping Mariana and Luca. Searching for the Ballon d'Or and keeping secrets from *everyone*."

Archie hadn't been happy Pen and Quin chose not to tell him all they knew about the mystery of the golden ball.

Quin hesitated, then said, "If you hadn't helped Pen with SPYder, we wouldn't have known Mariana's family was in trouble, or even met Luca."

Archie laughed and threw his hands into the air. "So I'm not blameless."

"But," Quin added, smiling. "Even though we got in trouble, and we didn't know searching for the trophy meant getting wrapped up with Daniel da Silva's deal with criminals, I don't regret it. Luca got the trophy back and Mariana and her family are safe now."

Archie nodded slowly. "True. Although, maybe we can keep fewer secrets from each other in the future." He punched Quin a little hard in the shoulder. Quin punched him back.

$$\rho$$

Yellow, orange, and purple lights hung from the bleachers, doorways, and anywhere else Pen and Eileen were able to reach. Their lights cast an eerie glow over St. Mary's gym, transforming it from a boring, smelly gym to a spooky autumn night. Carved pumpkins grinned crookedly on the refreshments table. Pen stood behind it, serving sodas and sweets to the fifth graders too scared to go farther into the gym, fearing they might have to dance.

The eighth graders ruled the dance floor, with some sixth and seventh graders mixed in. Pen searched the crowd for Michael and Mariana's blond hair. Both had dressed as pro soccer players. Mariana wore one of Luca's old jerseys and Michael had his sky blue Manchester City jersey on. Pen happened to know it matched his eyes perfectly. She couldn't find the pair in the crowd.

"They're dancing in the middle," Eileen said as she handed an orange soda nearly fizzing over the top of the cup to Dennis Leary. He gave her a dazed grin and stuttered thanks.

"Who?" Pen cut more brownies and set them on napkins.

"You know who," Eileen said and gave her a funny look. "Michael."

She rolled her eyes, which were accentuated by thick swathes of green eye shadow. Eileen carefully adjusted the scarf tied around her hair and straightened the beaded necklaces on her chest. Pen supposed Eileen thought all gypsies wore as much makeup and jewelry as possible. She didn't tell Eileen she'd seen real gypsies on her travels with Kostas and they didn't really look like that.

"I'm glad Michael asked Mariana to the dance," Pen

said, and she almost meant it. She was glad Mariana had something to take her mind off her father. Daniel da Silva had been released from police custody but ordered to return to Brazil. Mariana's mother had refused to go and kept Mariana with her. The Brazilian girl had hardly smiled or lifted her eyes from her books all week, although, she had worked with Pen to finish their American Revolution project, a detailed report on the spy craft of the Culper Spy Ring, including a coded message. The girls planned on handing out the message to everyone in class and decoding it together.

Pen tugged the sleeve of her dress up. It was one her grandmother had chosen for her in Mexico. The sleeves were set wide on her shoulders and the neckline plunged more than Pen was comfortable with, but Mamá had pinned her hair up and held it there with a red rose clip. "You look like a Spanish flamenco dancer," she'd said.

"That's what I told Abuela when she bought it." Pen smoothed the red dress with its white trim and fluffy skirt. It was the closest thing to a costume she had, except, of course, for her soccer jerseys.

A light flashed across the gym, and Anna's familiar laugh rang out. Pen looked at the photo booth where Quin was in his element. It'd been his idea to set up the booth with a black sheet and take photos of his classmates. Anna and Pen helped cut out the fake mustaches the students could hold up, and Ms. Morgan and Mr. Hardy added a collection of strange hats and scarves. The line for photos stretched nearly to the gym door.

Anna adjusted one of the lights spotlighting a group of four students and Quin's flash popped again. He wore one of Abuelito's old straw hats jauntily cocked on his head and a skinny tie he'd yanked out of Dad's closet. Pen smiled as he gestured for the group to ham it up and snapped another picture.

"Hey Penhead."

Mariana and Michael stood in front of the table, both

looking a little warm and flustered.

"*Está quente.*" Mariana grinned at Michael's baffled look. "It's hot," she said, fanning her neck. Pen handed her an orange soda. "*Obrigada.*" Mariana shot her a grateful look and Pen got the feeling she was thanking her for more than the soda.

"*De nada,*" Pen replied, and meant it. It was okay if Michael wanted to be with Mariana. She'd rather have Mariana for a friend, especially since her best friend now seemed so interested in her twin brother.

"You look different," Michael said, bringing Pen's attention sharply back. "I mean, you look—"

"Beautiful. Both of you," Mariana said, including Eileen in the compliment.

"Yeah," Michael echoed. "That."

"I have an idea," Eileen said. "Let's all take a picture together."

Pen opened her mouth to say no thank you, she didn't need a picture with Eileen Esposito, but she remembered just in time if not for Eileen seeing the man in black grab her and Quin and running to tell Ms. Morgan, Pen might not be at the dance. Pen closed her mouth firmly.

"*Sim,*" Mariana said. "I would like a photo to remember all of you."

"Remember?" Pen cried.

"Mariana's going to Spain to live with Luca." Michael looked happy he'd been the first to know this news. "She's going to try out for Atletico Madrid. The women's team, I mean." He gazed at Mariana with the same awe he had on his face when he'd learned Luca was her uncle.

Mariana's cheeks flushed pink. Pen sighed. Even dressed as a soccer player and sweating in a gym, Mariana was the picture of beauty. But she was more than that. She was Pen's friend.

"But you can't," Pen protested. "What about the rest of the season? And school?"

"Luca wants Mamãe and me closer to him," Mariana

explained. "And until Mamãe and Papai get back to-gether..." She stopped and blinked back a few tears.

Pen flushed. "I think that's wonderful, Mariana. You'll be close to Luca and get to see him play all the time."

Michael nodded enthusiastically. "And you'll be playing professionally, too. I know you'll make the team."

"You will," Pen said. "You're the best forward I've ever seen." She gave Michael an evil grin, but he only nodded.

"It's true. You're the best girl forward around." He shot that evil grin right back at Pen and she stuck out her tongue and laughed.

The four of them walked across the gym to Quin and Anna.

"Can you find another photographer?" Pen called.

"I can take the picture," a small voice piped up. Dennis Leary had trailed them across the gym. Quin handed the camera a little reluctantly to Dennis and showed him how to properly frame the picture. Then the six of them—Pen, Quin, Mariana, Michael, Anna, and Eileen, stood in front of the Fall Fest backdrop.

Mariana grabbed a sombrero and set it on Michael's head. She added a stylish scarf to her own outfit, then draped a black feather boa across Pen's shoulders. Pen laughed and handed Quin and Anna mustaches. Then she grabbed the last prop, a pirate hat, and plopped it on Eileen's head. "Thanks for following me," she whispered. "I mean, that last time at the park. Not the other times."

Eileen nodded. "You're welcome. And sorry I ruined SPYder for you when I told Ms. Morgan about it."

Pen shrugged. "Don't worry about it. I think I've had enough of mysteries for awhile."

"Smile," Dennis called out. The camera flashed before they were ready.

"Hey! Tell us before you take it," they all cried out.

"Sorry," Dennis called. "Are you ready?"

"What should we say on the count of three?" Quin asked. "Cheese?"

Michael shook his head. "Too boring."

"I know." Pen whispered to the other five and they all laughed.

"One-two-three," Dennis counted.

And at three, the camera flashed and the six friends shouted together.

About the Author

Kimberly S. Mitchell loves journeys, real or imagined. She has hiked the Inca Trail, walked into Panama on a rickety wooden bridge, and once missed the last train of the night in Paris. She believes magic can be found in life and books, loves to watch the stars appear, and still dreams of backpacking the world. Now she writes adventures to send her characters on journeys, too. She is the author of the *Pen & Quin: International Agents of Intrigue* series. Find out more at KSMitchell.com.

ACKNOWLEDGMENTS

Thank you, reader, for picking up the second book in the *Pen & Quin: International Agents of Intrigue* series. If this is your first mystery with the twins, I hope you'll read their previous adventure in *The Mystery of the Painted Book*, also available from Vinspire Publishing.

A book is always a collaboration. Thank you to Matthew, Georgia, and Cheryl for your time spent with Pen & Quin perfecting the story. Thank you Lindsay for being a first reader and your insight into the twins' personalities. Good thing you have a lot of experience being a twin!

Thank you to author Kristin L. Gray for reading and loving the book. Thank you Leticia Rueda for your keen eye on the Portuguese and Mariana's character. Thank you to Donna Feyen of More Than A Review for your early read and positive review of *The Mystery of the Golden Ball.*

And, of course, thank you to David for always supporting me on this crazy writing journey.

The author gratefully acknowledges trademark of the following:

Trademark Uses for Pen & Quin: International Agents of Intrigue - The Mystery of the Golden Ball

BOSTON RED SOX BASEBALL CLUB LIMITED PARTNERSHIP COMPOSED OF HAYWOOD C. SULLIVAN, A U.S. CITIZEN

AND JRY CORPORATION, A DELAWARE CORPORATION LIMITED PARTNERSHIP MASSACHUSETTS FENWAY PARK 4

YAWKEY WAY BOSTON MASSACHUSETTS 02215

REAL MADRID CLUB DE FUTBOL CORPORATION SPAIN Concha Espina, nº1 Madrid SPAIN 28036

DEAR READER

If you enjoyed reading the second book book in *Pen & Quinn's* adventures, *The Mystery of the Golden Ball*, I would appreciate it if you would help others enjoy this book, too. Here are some of the ways you can help spread the word:

Lend it. This book is lending enabled so please share it with a friend.

Recommend it. Help other readers find this book by recommending it to friends, readers' groups, book clubs, and discussion forums.

Share it. Let other readers know you've read the book by positing a note to your social media account and/or your Goodreads account.

Review it. Please tell others why you liked this book by reviewing it on your favorite ebook site.

Everything you do to help others learn about my book is greatly appreciated!

Kimberly Mitchell

Plan Your Next Escape!
What's Your Reading Pleasure?

Whether it's captivating historical romance, intriguing mysteries, young adult romance, illustrated children's books, or uplifting love stories, Vinspire Publishing has the adventure for you!

For a complete listing of books available, visit our website at www.vinspirepublishing.com.

Like us on Facebook at www.facebook.com/VinspirePublishing

Follow us on Twitter at www.twitter.com/vinspire2004

and follow our blog for details of our upcoming releases, giveaways, author insights, and more! www.vinspirepublishingblog.com.

We are your travel guide to your next adventure!

CPSIA information can be obtained
at www.ICGtesting.com
Printed in the USA
BVHW070115080920
588282BV00001B/47